R.c ≠ CB   DISc

Please return / renew by date shown.
You can renew it at:
norlink.norfolk.gov.uk
or by telephone: 0344 800 8006
Please have your library card & PIN ready

25 NOV

5 7 11

28. JUL 11.

Starr

2

THE LIBERATORS

When General Grant Westerly of the defeated Confederate Army arrives home he finds his parents murdered and his house a ruin. Only Joseph remains, to tell him about the terrible slaughter that had occurred at the hands of five deserters from the Union forces. When Grant and Joseph pursue the vengeance trail, heading south and then north through Indian country, hardship and danger are their constant companions. Only their determination and fighting skills can bring the murderers to justice.

BRETT LANDRY

THE LIBERATORS

Complete and Unabridged

LINFORD
Leicester

First published in Great Britain in 2000

Originally printed in paperback as
Vengeance Trail by James S. Farrow

First Linford Edition
published 2010

British Library CIP Data

Landry, Brett, *1919 –*
    The liberators.- -(Linford western library)
    1. Western stories.
    2. Large type books.
    I. Title II. Series
    III. Farrow, James S., *1919 –* Vengeance trail
    823.9'14–dc22

    ISBN 978–1–44480–090–6

Published by
F. A. Thorpe (Publishing)
Anstey, Leicestershire

Set by Words & Graphics Ltd.
Anstey, Leicestershire
Printed and bound in Great Britain by
T. J. International Ltd., Padstow, Cornwall

This book is printed on acid-free paper

1

He came out of the twilight, a tall man on a grey gelding, and both man and horse were spattered and grimed with mud and the marks of travel. Like the horse the man was grey, grey uniform, grey hat, grey trousers thrust into the tops of boots, once polished black but now grey with dirt. His face too was grey, drawn and strained with the ghastly pallor of utter fatigue, and as the tired horse jolted over the pitted and torn surface of the winding dirt road, its rider swayed and at times almost seemed on the verge of falling from the saddle.

At such times he would catch himself, jerking as though waking from sleep, and for a time would ride with practised ease, his hands light on the reins, his grey eyes beneath the shadow of his wide-brimmed hat alert and

1

questing as he stared into the thickening darkness. But such moments of awareness did not last long. As the horse stumbled its weary way onwards, he would relax, his shoulders would stoop, his eyes would half-close and, imperceptibly, he would sink back into the coma of a man who has ridden too hard for too long, and stay that way until some sudden jolt would jerk him awake again.

A mist began lifting from the ground as the night grew older, a thin, white mist which hid the shattered, moonlit desolation through which he rode, and because of the tiredness or because of the mist he seemed to see the countryside as it once had been, as he remembered it more than four long years ago.

Then the mansions had been white and proud, the windows filled with glass, the columns untouched by smoke and flame. Then the fields had been lush with cotton and cane and the voices of the working slaves had echoed across the valley as they sat around their fires and sang the old, plaintive songs which had somehow always stirred him with a sense of shame. Then there had been peace and arrogance and the supreme conviction that this way of life, the Southern way, would last for ever. Even when war had come it had seemed unreal, a thing which would be soon over and the Confederacy established for all time to maintain the gracious living to which the plantation owners had become accustomed.

Then Sherman had marched through Georgia and the dream was broken like the brittle thing it had been.

Sherman, with his army of blue-uniformed Unionists, marching and destroying, teaching the proud South a lesson it would never forget, shattering the power of the Confederacy and disrupting the entire economy of landowners and planters, slave owners and traders. Sherman, who had freed the slaves with the power of his cannon

— but who had brought ruin to those who opposed him.

And now of the glorious South nothing was left but destroyed houses, empty fields, landless soldiers, masterless slaves and the arrogant, impatient forces of the Union troops.

The horse stumbled and the tall man, far gone in his coma, swayed and almost fell. He jerked awake to the harsh glare of light and sat, blinking, as a bearded soldier thrust a lantern into his face.

'Hold it there, you.' The soldier spat as he recognized the Confederate uniform. 'A Johnny Reb, by cracky! And on a horse too.' He spat again and jerked his thumb. 'Step down, rebel. From here you finish your journey on foot.'

The tall man didn't move. He just sat, staring down at the soldier who had halted him, and now his grey eyes were alert as he stared at his surroundings. A tent had been erected at one side of the road and a small fire smouldered beneath a boiling cauldron of stew. A lantern, twin to the one the soldier held, hung on a pole, and across the road a light hurdle made a rough road-block.

It was a check-point, one of hundreds scattered in the war-torn South, and the tall man sighed as he lifted his left hand to a pocket.

'My name is General Grant Westerly,' he said without emotion. 'I am on my way home from the military hospital at Fort Main. I have a pass signed by Commander Jelks and his order to all Union troops to afford me safe passage.'

'Is that so?' The soldier spat again and rubbed his bearded mouth with the filthy sleeve of his tunic. 'Fort Main, you said?'

'Yes.'

'That's ours. How come a dirty Reb was at Fort Main?'

'I was a prisoner,' explained Grant curtly. 'I was wounded and captured and have only recently been released.'

5

He took papers from his pocket. 'Here is my pass.'

For all the notice the soldier took of the document Grant could as well have shown him an empty hand. Instead he walked around the horse, sniffing at its jaded condition, feeling its fetlocks and prodding its withers. Finally, after his examination, he stared up at the tall man again.

'This horse ain't much, Reb. You got any money?'

'A little. Why?'

'Union money?'

'No, Confederate.'

'Too bad.' The soldier hawked and spat. 'If you had real money I'd maybe have let you go with the horse. Seeing how you ain't I guess that I'll have to ask you to step down and get moving.'

'And if I refuse?'

'Try it.' Something animal gleamed in the soldier's eyes and his hands shifted on his bayonet-tipped carbine. 'Just you try riding off, Reb. Just you try.'

It wasn't a threat but an invitation, and Grant knew that the soldier was itching to plunge his bayonet into living flesh. For a moment the tall man hesitated between making a break for it or obeying the soldier's command. Without a horse he wouldn't have a chance of finishing his journey, and yet if he tried to escape the soldier would shoot him dead.

He was just about to obey the soldier when a man came into the circle of lantern-light.

He was an officer, a youthful captain, his uniform fresh and clean, his boyish face reflecting his military pride. He stared at Grant and then at the papers he still held in his hand. Taking them he turned to the soldier.

'What's the trouble?'

'Trouble?' The soldier shrugged. 'Nothing I can't handle, Captain. Why don't you just go back into your tent and leave it to me?'

'You forget yourself!' The boyish captain stiffened as he glared at the soldier. For a long moment their eyes met, those of the soldier challenging those of the young captain, then, with something which sounded like a curse, he shrugged and slouched back to the pole bearing the lantern. The young officer sighed and looked up at the tall man.

'Captain Delton at your service, sir,' he said courteously. 'Will you join me in my tent while I examine your papers?'

'Is that a command or an invitation?'

'An invitation.' Delton glanced at the jaded horse. 'Both of you would be better for the rest. I have a little feed to spare, your horse can have it, and I think that you yourself could do with a plate of stew.' He hesitated. 'The war is over, General. Will you do me the courtesy of sharing a meal?'

Grant nodded.

The stew was good, the wine was better, and the old brandy better still. Delton, his head still full of old military etiquette, had considered it still an honour to entertain a general of the losing side, and Grant, though he had long lost his idealism, did nothing to disillusion the young man. Delton at the moment offered the very things Grant needed most. Food, information and safety. Despite his hate of the Union forces. Grant was intelligent enough to use the opportunity to hand and skilfully he pumped the young man dry.

It was worse, far worse than Grant had ever dreamed.

'The South is ruined,' said Delton with simple conviction. 'In a way you were lucky to have missed the actual march from Atlanta. That was bad, but it was war, and many things are expected to happen in war. Now the war is over, but in a way things are even worse.'

'I've heard the stories,' said Grant. 'Union troops running wild, deserting so as to loot and destroy. Are they true?'

'Unfortunately, yes.' Delton poured more brandy and didn't look his guest in the eyes. 'You saw the type of men I have beneath me. Dirty, brutal, drunken swine for the most part. The scum of the North who saw a chance for wealth in war. They aren't soldiers, General, not as we know soldiers, but what can we do? The best men were killed during the four years of war. The march from Atlanta demoralized those who were left. You can't really blame them, the orders were to destroy everything in sight, and the army went hog-wild.'

'Yes,' said Grant, and a muscle began to twitch high on one cheek.

'We'd been in the field for weeks before the final break-through,' said Delton. 'We were half-starved, ill, sick with the stench of blood and powder. Suddenly we were on the move and all any of us could think of was to kill and burn and tear down so that this terrible thing could never happen again.' He shuddered and his eyes as he stared at the tent wall were filled with the smouldering shadows of things better left forgotten.

'We burned the plantation houses and freed the slaves,' he said quietly, and to Grant it seemed as if the young man was talking to himself. 'That was policy, that was why we were fighting the war, that was a thing which had to be done. Break the wealth of the South and rid this land from the threat of war forever.'

'Yes,' said Grant again, and stared at his glass.

'We had swine among us,' whispered the captain. 'They weren't satisfied with doing what had to be done. They got rotten drunk and torched everything they could find. They roasted entire families, robbed and killed, ran across the country like a plague. We shot those we found and could prove had been looting, but then we had to stop even that. Nothing could prevent them from gorging their hate on the Confederacy. Nothing.'

'Are you trying to convince yourself or me?' said Grant evenly. He stared at the young officer. 'I was at Pikes Field when I was captured and that was before the final break-through. I've been a prisoner in Fort Main and have only just been released. They gave me a horse, my uniform, a safe conduct and that was all. They left me to travel five hundred miles. Are you going to stop me now?'

'No.'

'That soldier of yours was going to steal my horse.'

'I know.'

'Can't you control your men?'

'When I'm around I can.' Delton shrugged and abruptly drained his glass. 'I'm one man, General, with a dozen prison-scum who are supposed to be taking my orders. If I look twice at some of them they desert. If they see a chance of making money, they desert. If they just feel like it, they desert. All the time they desert and there's nothing I can do about it. How can I? With the South in the way it is all they have to do is to sell their rifles, get rid of their uniforms and call themselves carpetbaggers.

Most of them grab what they can find and then head West. Once into Texas or across the border they are as safe as a man can be.' The young officer shrugged again. 'Don't think I like it, General, but that's how it is. When things have settled a little the army will get back to what it should be, but at the moment some men are literally getting away with murder.'

'And you?'

'I'm a West Point graduate,' said Delton stiffly. 'I don't like what is happening and I'm doing what I can to alter it. Personally I'll be glad when my transfer comes through and I get away from this territory. I'm a cavalry man and I'm not happy trying to act policeman.' He smiled and refilled the glasses. 'Let's forget it. Drink deep, General, and tell me what you thought of the war.'

'Later,' said Grant. His eyes were thoughtful. 'I've a journey to make and I want to get some things clear. How bad are things around Freeman County?'

'Freeman County?' Delton looked thoughtful. 'Not so good. Why?'

'Do you know anything of a big white Colonial house? They call it 'Green Shutters' and it rests about a half a mile from the road.' Grant leaned forward in his anxiety. 'Have you heard anything about that house?'

'Nothing.' Delton shifted uncomfortably on his chair. 'I'm fairly new in this region and one house looks just like another to me. Freeman County is about fifty miles south-west from here and my patrols don't go that far.' He looked at the tall man. 'Is it important?'

'I think so.'

'I see.' Delton bit at his lower lip. 'I can't help you, General, I'm sorry. I'm not going to soft-syrup you, either. Things are pretty bad all over, worse in some parts than others, but still pretty bad. You had folks down that way?'

'Yes.' Grant drained his brandy, fighting the tearing impatience which made him want to jump to his feet, mount his horse and gallop into the darkness. He could feel his muscles trembling with the desire to get up and get moving, but despite his impatience he knew that no good would come of mad haste.

The gelding was jaded and could travel no more than a few miles before collapsing. It was dark, he wasn't too sure of the roads, and at any time a Union patrol could halt and detain him. He himself was at the end of his tether. Still weak from his wounds, out of condition from his harsh imprisonment, drugged with fatigue, he was in no condition for further travel. Meeting the young, idealistic officer was the best thing which could have happened to him, but Grant, listening to his talk, felt like jumping up and running into the night.

It had been so long.

Four years at least. Four long, weary years in which he had changed from boy into man, risen from private to general, four years of blood and hate and hardship, with his strength and emotions scarred and tempered by the fires of war.

Tiredly he closed his eyes and, as happened so often, he saw again the white, sun-painted portico, the tall windows, the graceful columns and Virginia creeper of the house in which he had been born. He saw too his mother's face, his father, old, stern, and yet softening towards his youngest son. His brother, three years dead now, and his sister who had withered from typhoid to die in a hospital far to the east.

Four years, and for the past ten months there had been no news.

He started dreaming again that he was riding, riding, riding as he had done for the past week, not stopping for other than food or to rest the horse. He opened his eyes and stared at Delton leaning over him.

'What is it?'

'You were crying out in your sleep.'

'Was I?' Grant took a deep breath. 'Dreams, think nothing of them.'

'No.' Delton took a cigar case from his pocket and handed a slim cylinder to Grant. 'Smoke?'

'Thanks.' Grant rolled the cigar between thumb and forefinger, inhaled its fragrance, then lit it at the flame of the lantern and filled his lungs before exhaling twin plumes through his nostrils. 'Sorry about that, I didn't mean to fall asleep.'

'You called out,' said Delton, and he flushed. 'Listen, I don't want to pry, but I want you to know that I can appreciate how you must feel. I'm an officer of the Union Army. I was your enemy. Now I am only your fellow countryman. I'd like to believe that you look at it that way too.'

'I'd like to,' said Grant, and dragged at the cigar. 'But maybe it would come easier if I sat where you are sitting without thinking of the folks who are dead, the houses which have been burned, the fields empty, the cats and dogs living where once men and women lived. I've seen too many young boys smashed into the dirt and I've seen too much hate. I'd like to forget, but forgetting doesn't come easy to a beaten man.'

'I know.'

'You don't know. You can't know. I — ' Grant broke off and stared at the glowing tip of his cigar. 'Hell! I'm talking too much.'

'Talking can help,' said Delton. 'Perhaps.'

'Look,' said Delton. 'Maybe I'm crazy and maybe you'd be crazy too, but there's something I've got to say. I've heard of Freeman County, and from what I hear there's a gang of toughs wandering around and stirring up hell. You're a Rebel, still in Reb uniform, and if they find you they won't be gentle. I've a set of civilians you can have and — '

'No.' Grant shook his head. 'I left home a soldier and that's the way I intend going back. I'm not ashamed of my uniform, what I am and what I did.' He stared at the young officer. 'Are you trying to tell me that a man isn't safe even at his own home?'

'If he has a home,' said Delton, and suddenly became busy with glasses and brandy. 'I told you that it was pretty bad.'

'You said that before.' Grant blinked his sore eyes and wished that he didn't feel so tired. His entire body ached and it was getting hard to focus his eyes. As he watched Delton seemed to waver and when he moved it was as if he just changed position without moving in between. A sudden pain between his fingers made him realize that he had forgotten his cigar. It had burned down until the hot ash had seared his skin.

'Drink this,' said Delton, and Grant smelt the pungent odour of brandy. 'Drink it down and go to sleep. You can have my cot for tonight and I'll call you early in the morning. Drink up now. Drink and relax.'

'No.' Grant struggled to his feet. 'I can't wait. I've got to get moving, to find out, to — ' He lurched and abruptly was sitting down again. Delton moved across the tent, looked outside, then came back again.

'You won't be going anywhere tonight. Your horse is dead to the world. It would take a cannon to wake him and he'd not carry you a mile.' He picked up the brandy again. 'Come on, General. Drink this and relax.'

This time Grant didn't argue.

2.

Morning came and with it the sun which drove away the mist and dried the dew from the grass, the moisture from the trees, and lent a false air of well-being to the world in general. Beneath the bright light the desolation looked different, not so utter, almost as if the empty fields would soon be busy again and that the whole thing was but a fragment out of time, not real, not permanent, merely something that would pass as swiftly as it had come.

It was only when Grant saw the ruined mansions that the true position registered again.

He felt better, far better than he had for too long how. Delton had fed him, rested him, and fed him again. Now, with the hot stew filling his stomach and the warmth of the brandy taking the chill from his bones, Grant faced the world with a new confidence. Between his thighs the gelding, also refreshed, stepped out with more spring and greater care. But Grant resisted the temptation to spur the horse into a gallop. If he did that the poor beast would run until he burst his heart, but Grant knew that he would not be able to run for long.

Delton had done more than given them food.

Arms were forbidden to all members of the Confederate Army and Grant knew that Delton had broken military law in doing what he had done. At the last, just before Grant had mounted, the young officer had called him into the tent and there had handed him a pistol. Grant could feel it now, resting against his stomach beneath his tunic. A long-barrelled Navy pistol, six chambered and each chamber holding an ounce of lead. Six lives if the man holding the pistol knew how to use it.

And Grant had been taught in a hard school.

All the day the tall man rode along the rutted path. Night fell and he rested beneath a great magnolia tree, fireless and foodless, sitting half asleep but able to leap into alertness at the slightest sound. Dawn came and again he rode into the brightening sunlight, and now, despite his caution, he began to meet others on the road.

Coloured people mostly. The freed slaves from the plantations, wandering without aim or purpose, uprooted from the only homes they had ever known, feeling both elated and sorry at losing the masters who, while being their support, had too often been their tormentors.

Others mingled with the ex-slaves, the civilian-suited carpetbaggers who had swarmed in the wake of the victorious army with their promise of 'forty acres and a mule' to every freed slave who voted as directed. A promise both impossible and unintended.

Evening darkened the sky and finally Grant swung off the road and began to ride down an overgrown drive lined with trees and heavy with the scent of magnolia. Now, for the first time in days, he spurred the gelding. Metal rang as the horse responded and, with mounting impatience, Grant galloped down the drive which led to his home.

It would be at the end of the drive, a tall, stately house in the Colonial manner, its walls dulled a little, perhaps, but with its great doors still wide in welcome as they had always been. The house slaves would be at the back, the field slaves in their huts towards the edge of the plantation. Servants would meet him, take the reins and tend to his horse, while others, their white teeth flashing against their dark skins, would greet him with permitted familiarity, fetch him a tall mint julep, fetch water for him to lave his hands, prepare a bath and lay out clean linen.

And his parents would be there too. A little older, a little careworn at the loss of son and daughter, but all the more eager to greet him, their sole surviving child.

That was the dream. The thing he had carried with him for four years through hell and death and hardship.

The truth —

He dragged at the reins savagely, incredulously, and as the horse shuddered to a halt his grey eyes widened with horror.

No house. No parents. No slaves. Nothing.

Where had stood the house now rested a tumbled heap of fire-blackened brick. A wall, half destroyed, remained standing, its whiteness overlaid with the mark of the inferno which had destroyed the dwelling. The columns had toppled and lay like sticks of charred wood, the ground was scarred, the houses of the house slaves had vanished as though they had never been.

Grant sat and stared at the desolation. Deep within himself he knew that he was not surprised. Somehow he had expected this, and to actually see it was a shock he hadn't expected. The house was gone. The only home he had ever known had been burned by drunken looters, for it was far away from the bloody trail of Sherman's triumphal progress, on his savage march from Atlanta through Georgia, which had split the South in two and destroyed the Confederacy. There had been destruction then, but it was calculated, military destruction, not the drunken brutishness of criminals in blue.

Grimly he rode forward, his grey eyes bleak and his mouth a thin gash across the strained tension of his face. The house was gone, but houses could be rebuilt. His parents —

Something moved at the edge of his vision and he reined, his hand slipping beneath his tunic. The dying sun gleamed on the pistol he jerked from his waistband, and his voice, when he called out, had all the iron of command.

'Halt! Move and I fire!'

Silence. The wind, rising from the west, stirred the leaves of the trees and sighed like the voices of long-dead ghosts through the shattered walls of the house. Grant sat in the saddle, his eyes narrowed as he tried to penetrate the darkness beneath the trees.

'I see you,' he called. 'Step forward.'

Again the wind played among the leaves, and the shadows remained unbroken. Grant thinned his lips as his bluff failed, then slipping from the saddle he ran towards where he had glimpsed the suggestion of movement.

And almost died in a hail of lead.

His own weakness saved him, that and an unseen root which caught at his foot. He staggered and fell just as the gun roared, and so close were the bullets that he felt something twitch the hat from his head. In the shocking silence following the report he heard the sound of a man racing through the undergrowth, and he levelled his own pistol ready to fire.

Grant eased the pressure on the

trigger as he caught a glimpse of a running shape.

'Joseph,' he called. 'Joe! Damn your black hide, stop or I'll fire!'

The man halted so abruptly that he almost fell. He stared at the tall man behind him as if at a ghost, then as Grant walked up to him he began to shake and tremble, great beads of sweat glistening on his ebon features.

'Master!' he gasped. 'It's the young master! And I tried to shoot you dead with the old gun.'

'You almost made a good job of it,' said Grant drily. Now that he had found human companionship some of the sickening horror of seeing the house in ruin had left him. He knew that it wasn't certain knowledge he was afraid of, but the terrible uncertainty of not knowing. He smiled at the man, glad that it was Joseph he had found and not one of the other, almost illiterate field hands. Joseph had been the house butler back in the old days and his English was as Grant's own.

'What happened, Joseph?' he asked. 'What made you try to kill me? Where are the others?'

'It's getting dark,' said Joseph quietly. 'Your horse is tired, master, and should be attended to. You yourself look ill. We had better get things done before we talk.'

It made sense, such good sense that Grant didn't even have time to wonder at the note of assurance in the man's voice. Joe was right, he was tired, and not even his brief rest with Delton had done anything to more than freshen his awareness. Dully he watched as he attended to the horse.

He slipped the saddle from the animal and hid it beneath some stones at the foot of the ruined wall. The horse he took inside a lean-to, a flimsy thing of brushwood propped at an angle in a ruined corner. He fetched a bucket filled with water and a great armful of sweet-smelling hay. The gelding, after drinking noisily, munched at the hay and, as Joe led Grant towards the undergrowth surrounding the house, he knew that soon the horse would be asleep.

It had grown quite dark by this time, and Grant followed his guide more by touch than anything else. He felt soft dirt beneath his feet, a shadow loomed ahead, and as Joe threw open a door, fitful firelight showed a small hut redolent of cooking and with a crude bed made of piled rags in one corner.

Joe shut the door, propped it with a length of wood and with grim determination began to clean and load an old-fashioned blunderbuss which Grant recognized as having once hung on the wall of the gun room.

'Is that what you shot at me with, Joe?'

'Yes, sir. I picked it up as we walked past the place where I had dropped it.' Joe bent to his work, his dark skin shining in the dull glow of the fire. Grant waited until he had rammed home the powder, the wadding, and an assortment of scraps of lead, iron and brass. The weapon, though obsolete, was still capable of inflicting terrible injuries and, at short range, could literally blow a man to shreds.

'Why did you want to kill me, Joe?'

'I didn't, sir,' Joe said quickly. 'That is, I didn't want to kill you. I thought you were a prowler, a looter, someone who was looking for trouble.'

'You get many like that?'

'Too many.' There was a hard bleakness in Joe's voice which Grant found hard to understand. His memories of the butler were of a soft-voiced, obsequious servant seemingly incapable of any act of violence or aggression. Grant shifted uncomfortably, his instincts fighting his training. Instinct screamed for him to ask what had happened, to demand a recounting of what had become of his parents and the events leading to the destruction of the house. His training made it difficult for him to treat the man as other than a slave, a servant before whom a superficial dignity was all-important.

Instinct won.

'Tell me what happened, Joe,' he demanded. 'My parents, where are they? The house, what happened?'

'Your parents are dead.'

It wasn't so much what he said as the way he said it that made Grant stare at Joe in amazement. His voice was not that of a servant, rather it was that of a man filled with a terrible bitterness and pain, a pain so great that he thought nothing of hurting others. Then the shock registered.

'Dead! Both of them dead!'

'Yes, sir,' said Joe, and then before Grant could speak: 'I'm sorry, but it is best to tell you quickly. A sharp wound heals fastest.'

Grant nodded. The servant was right, bad news was best broken quickly, bluntly, and without mistaken gentleness. It hurt, but, as Joe had said, it was better that way. In effect it was the stopping of wonderment and the anxiety which not knowing brought. His parents were dead, and that was the end of it. Almost.

'How — ?' Grant swallowed. 'What happened?'

'I'm ashamed,' burst out the man suddenly. 'I'm ashamed of what I am and what I did. I thought of revenge, but when the chance came I could think of nothing but forgiveness. I forgot my hate in horror. I — '

He caught his breath, and with shocking abruptness he was on the floor, his arms around Grant's legs, his face twisted as the tears rolled down his cheeks.

'Forgive me, sir. Forgive me as you would be forgiven. I did not dream that liberation would be the thing it is.'

'Liberation?' Grant shook his head, not understanding.

'That is how I thought of it,' said Joe fiercely. 'I and all those like me. We welcomed the war, you will never know how much we welcomed it. To us it promised freedom and only a slave can know what that word means. We thought of the Union Army as our saviours.' He caught his breath again and when he spoke he seemed to be whispering as if to himself.

'Fire and rum and madness, that was our liberation.'

'Tell me!' Savagely Grant gripped the man by the shoulders and shook him as though he had been a child. 'Damn you, Joe! Tell me!'

'Yes, sir,' said Joe calmly. 'I shall tell you.' He paused, and in the firelight Grant could see the grey thickly sprinkling his hair. He frowned, trying for some reason to remember if he had ever noticed it before, then forgot the trifle as Joe began to speak.

'I was born a slave,' he said simply, 'and my parents and their parents, and their parents were born in captivity. My father was beaten to death for stealing an apple; my sister was branded on both cheeks; my mother was sold down the river, and my two brothers were marked as cattle are marked before being whipped to death in the fields. I, of them all, was fortunate in being sold when a boy to your father. I was even more fortunate in being trained as a house servant and finally obtaining the position of butler.'

Grant nodded impatiently.

'I was an abolitionist. I was a member of the underground railway, the organization which helped runaway slaves to reach the North and freedom. I have fed and helped many slaves to escape while I worked for your father. And I have hated slavery all my life!'

'Why?' Grant stared at the man in honest enquiry. 'You were a slave, yes, but you were well fed, well treated, well trained and looked after. Slavery is bad, perhaps, but without it you would have starved.'

'You do not know what it is to be a slave,' said Joe fiercely. 'To be little better than an animal, to be sold, whipped, scarred, branded and beaten at the whim of a master. If the war was justified by nothing else it was justified if it ends that hell on earth for my people.'

'I'm glad you think so,' said Grant heavily. 'The war was fought and we lost. Now no black man is a slave, all are free.' He laughed, curtly, bitterly. 'You are free — to starve.'

'We are free,' admitted Joe. He sighed. 'Try to understand how I felt when the Union Army finally turned the tide of war. Liberation was at hand, and when a party of the Union troops approached the house I welcomed them. Your father wanted to fight, but I saw to it that he didn't. He trusted me, sometimes I even think he liked me as a man, not as a slave, and together we surrendered the house to the soldiers.'

'And then?'

'They took possession. They ate what food we had and drunk until they were more like animals than men. Then one of them mentioned treasure. He said that there were valuables in the house. They took your mother's jewels and all the silver and gold they could find, but they weren't satisfied.' Joe stared down at his hands. 'They began to torture your mother so as to make your father give them his treasure.'

'What?' Grant clenched his hands until the nails dug into his palms. His face became moist with sweat and a great trembling shook every muscle of his body. He was thinking of his mother, a crowd of drunken swine, and a non-existent treasure.

'I tried to tell them that there was no treasure,' said Joe desperately. 'They cursed me, struck me, and flung me out of the house.' He bent his head and parted his hair. 'See, I bear the mark of the wound. I recovered only to see the house in flames and the soldiers drinking from bottles and firing at something lying on the ground. After they had gone I crawled towards it, it was the body of your father. I buried him beneath the big magnolia tree, which stood before the house.'

'And my mother?'

'I could find no trace of her. She must have perished in the flames.'

'I see.' Grant felt the muscle begin to

twitch high on one cheek. 'And the slaves?'

'They ran away carrying what they could and breaking what they couldn't. I alone am left.'

'Why did you stay, Joseph?'

'I had a duty,' said the man simply. 'I had done a great wrong and felt that somehow, some way, I must undo that wrong. I trusted men who were not to be trusted and, because of me, your parents died. So I stayed near the house hoping that one day you would return. You did, and I almost killed you.'

'You shot at me thinking I was one of the soldiers?'

'Yes.'

'Have any of them returned? Was that why you waited here?'

'Yes.'

'The same ones? Have they returned?'

'No.' Joseph stared at his hands. 'I learned after that those men were deserters from the Union Army, not really soldiers at all. They had enlisted to get away from trouble and saw the chance to make some easy money. They talked when they were drunk and I learned a lot, but by then it was too late to do anything to stop them. I have waited here for others like them, uniformed dogs who shame the uniform they wear. They come like wolves to see what they can loot. Three of them are buried at the edge of the plantation.'

'And now?'

'Now you are home again. I have guarded what little is left and it is yours. The house is gone but the land remains, and it is yours.'

'Not now it isn't,' said Grant grimly. 'You haven't heard what has been happening, Joseph. The plantations are being broken up, legally of course, but broken just the same. The victors are slamming unpayable taxes on all lands owned by the Confederates. We cannot pay, and so, quite legally, the land is seized and sold to Northern carpetbaggers. Without slaves to work the fields, without money to pay wages or taxes, I haven't a chance. I own nothing but the clothes I wear, my horse and what I can salvage from the ruins of the house. In a way, Joseph, you are far better off than I am. You have gained your freedom, while I have lost my home, my parents and everything I possess.'

'There are a few things I managed to save,' said Joseph. 'Some clothes, a little money, a few trinkets. I have a horse hidden in the brush and the men I shot carried weapons. You may be able to sell them for some money.'

Grant nodded, staring into the fire. He thought of Delton and what he had said about the men of his command. He thought of his parents and what had been done to them, and he thought of the futility of war. But he thought more of the men who had wantonly killed and burned for the sake of a drunken whim. Those men had not been soldiers, they had been criminals wearing Union blue, and the galling part of it all was that they would escape the consequences of their action. No one would be interested enough or brave enough to make them pay for their double murder. No one unless —

'You said that you heard those men talk,' said Grant casually. 'What did they say, what did they look like, what were their names?' He looked at Joseph, and something in his eyes made him recoil as from a venomous snake.

'You can't do it,' said Joe. 'You have too much to live for and it is wrong for a young man to live for revenge.'

'I'm waiting,' said Grant.

'Where would you find them? Where would you look?' Joe wrung his hands as if desperate at the emotions he had aroused. 'They could be anywhere, they could even be dead by now.'

'I'm still waiting.'

'There were five of them. One of them was a big man with a scar down one cheek, the left cheek, and the others called him Jud. One had a bullet-notched ear, a thin, small man with bad teeth, he was called Kent. The third was a fat man with hands like a woman, he had little beady black eyes and a high-pitched laugh, they called him Tiny, I don't know why.'

'And the others?'

'Twins. Both had the same mark tattooed on the backs of their left hands. They were called Roper, Fred and Sam Roper. They laughed often and spoke much in Spanish. They looked like men who had spent much of their time in the open.'

'I see.' Grant nodded, his memory filing away the facts. 'Did they say what they intended to do?'

'No.'

'No?' Grant frowned. 'Not even a word, a name? Did they talk as though they had known each other long? Did they talk as though they would work together again?' He leaned forward, his eyes intent. 'Did they?'

'From what they said they had broken out of prison together and had enlisted to throw off pursuit. They had deserted and were on their way to safety. They wanted to gather all the gold they could on their way. The fat man laughed as he talked about it, said something that it was a pity there were no banks worth robbing now that Confederate money was valueless. Another man, Kent I think, said that this beat gold mining. The Ropers were excellent riders and both wore pistols low on their hips.' Joe hesitated. 'They mentioned a name.'

'Yes?'

'Alamatri.'

'Alamatri,' repeated Grant slowly. 'It sounds as if it might be a place in Mexico.'

'That is what they said,' admitted Joseph. 'The fat man said something about being over the border would be safest for them.' He hesitated. 'I had thought of trying to find them.'

'Why?' asked Grant.

Joseph said nothing, but watching him the tall man could guess his reasons. He stared into the fire.

'We'll both go,' he said.

Joseph nodded.

3

Alamatri turned out to be a fly-blown town set in the scorpion-infested desert south of the Rio Grande. A crude huddle of tumbledown shacks, it had no permanence and no tradition. It looked what it was, a meeting place for those who carried what they owned and wanted nothing but a place to sleep, eat, gamble and get safely drunk. A corral sprawled at the edge of town, a tavern sold raw tequila and rawer whiskey, a hotel catered for those who wanted food, dispensing spicy tamales and soggy beans, and offering dubious accommodation to anyone with the price to hire one of the verminous rooms.

The place stank with the rotting sewage in the dirt streets, piles of garbage stood behind the clapboard dwellings, and all water came from a well carelessly sunk in the centre of the patio. It seemed as if the builders, overawed by the wide expanse of the surrounding desert, had deliberately refused to allow light and air to circulate between the houses. The place looked what it was and was as lawless as it looked.

Late one afternoon two horsemen rode slowly down the winding trail towards the apparently deserted town. Both wore the almost regulation garb of the frontier, thick shirts, jeans, high boots, leather jackets, wide-brimmed hats and neck scarves. Both were armed with pistol and knife, but while one carried a rifle in his saddle scabbard, the other had a shotgun.

Grant halted his mount at the top of a slight rise and stared thoughtfully at the huddle of shacks before him.

'Think this is it, Joe?'

'It should be,' said Joseph. 'They told us at the last town that Alamatri was about here.' He shifted in his saddle and touched the butt of his shotgun. 'I hope that this is it.'

'So do I,' said Grant emotionlessly. He had long lost his searing impatience to find and kill the men responsible for the murder of his parents. His resolve remained, but time and hardship had given him a fatalistic patience. Both he and Joseph had altered from the men they had been. Joseph, once the perfect servant, now thought and acted as the equal to any man living. Grant had encouraged him in that, addressing him as a friend and not as a servant, and as they had wandered on their long search over a thousand miles of broken terrain, each had learned much about the other.

'I can hardly believe that we've found it at last,' said Joe, 'At first it seemed so easy, just find a town in Mexico called Alamatri. How were we to know that it was on no map and unknown to most?'

'It has been a long time,' admitted Grant. Gently he touched his spurs to the sides of his horse. 'Let's see what we can find.'

Life became apparent as they approached

the town. A peon, hidden in the shadow of a building, lifted his head and stared at them as they passed. A man, chewing a straw and watching the horses in the corral, took the straw from his mouth, spat and then followed them with his eyes. A woman screamed to a couple of naked children playing in the dirt and swore after them in fluent Spanish, and a man, his olive skin and faded finery proclaiming him a gaucho from one of the huge haciendas of the South, laughed and called out to a woman peering from behind a tattered curtain.

Grant rode on, his face immobile, not betraying the fact that he, like Joseph, had understood every word the man had said.

Arriving at the saloon they dismounted, hitched their horses to the rail and entered the tavern. At first the contrast between the inner dimness to the glare of the sun outside made them blink and stand for a moment until their eyes adjusted to the gloom. When they could see clearly again they became aware of a crowd of men sprinkled with women, all of them staring at the newcomers, all tense and ready for action.

Then Grant strode across to the long bar, rapped on the scarred wood with a silver dollar, and life and normalcy returned to the patrons of the establishment.

'Tequila,' he ordered as the bartender, a squat, swarthy Mexican approached them. Grant watched as the man placed two glasses and a bottle on the counter, poured a generous helping of the potent spirit into each glass, downed his portion at a gulp and refilled the glasses immediately.

'You are thirsty, *señor*,' said the man in Spanish. 'A long ride, no?'

'Talk English,' snapped Grant. 'I don't cotton on to that monkey talk. You were saying?'

'It is hot, no?' The bartender smiled with a flash of gold-spotted teeth. 'The sun makes a man thirsty after a long ride. Did you have trouble crossing the river?'

48

'Did I?' Grant shrugged and sipped at his second drink. He knew that the bartender was trying to find out where he was from, and his question had been designed to that end. Ignoring the man, he stared about him at the people and furnishings of the tavern.

It was a replica of a thousand others scattered all over the West. A huge room ringed with a balcony and edged by a long counter. Half of the room was taken up with the gaming tables, faro, poker, blackjack, dice and a spinning wheel. The other half was bare, aside from a jangling piano set against one wall, and was filled by a hard-faced crowd of men, many with even harder-faced women. All the men were armed with pistols hanging low on their hips, many were bearded and most were burned almost black by the sun. They looked what they were, men living on the edge of the law, rough, tough, dangerous. Men who lived and died by the quickness of their fingers on the trigger.

Grant sighed as he looked at them, hoping that he would find one of the men whose description was burned in his memory, then as he saw no one fitting the pattern, listened to the bartender talking to Joe.

'Your friend he is touchy, no? Here it is the custom for a stranger to tell where he is from.' The bartender spread his hands. 'It is from no idle curiosity we wish to know, you understand, but men must be careful in these times.'

'Careful?' Joe shrugged and swallowed his drink. 'You talk to me about being careful?' He laughed with a flash of white teeth. 'Man! You don't know what you're saying.' He laughed again, a deep, rolling laugh which made men stare at him in sudden wonder. Joe snapped his fingers, and the Mexican, eager to please, refilled his glass.

'Drink, señor. Drink again. Tequila is good for a man's soul.'

'Tequila is good for a lot of things,' sniggered Joe, swaying a little. 'Man, but I'm strapped. Three days' riding

50

and the posse getting closer all the time. I — '

'Joe!' Grant turned and stared at his friend. 'Button your lip.'

'Sure,' Joe chuckled, and winked. 'Sure, but what the hell? We're among friends, aren't we?'

'Indeed yes, *señor*,' said the bartender. For some reason he seemed relieved at the man's slip. 'You are safe here. No Marshal, no Sheriff, no *Rurales* to bother you. Here you can rest and spend your gold and no man will harm you.' He tilted the bottle again. 'More tequila, *señor*.'

'Thanks.' Joe reached for the glass, and as he did so his elbow brushed against a man standing just behind him. It was an accident, a mere chance, but the man, half-drunk and scowling, swore and glared at him.

'Watch it,' he snapped. 'I don't want no dirty slave pawing me.'

'Slave?' Joe tensed and slowly put down his glass. He straightened, his eyes hard in the bleakness of his face, and watching him the crowd fell away so as to give the two men room.

'That's what I said,' snarled the man. He was bearded, dirty, his breath foul with stale liquor, He spat and fell into a half-crouch, the tips of his fingers brushing the butts of the twin guns he wore at his waist. 'If you don't like it do something about it.' He grinned, showing blackened snags of rotting teeth. 'Come on, slave, let's see if you can use that hog-leg you carry.'

'Take it easy,' wailed the bartender. 'Please, Bill, no trouble in here.'

'Shut your mouth,' snapped Bill. 'Keep talking and I'll run a spit through you and roast you over a fire. I'm talking to him.' His eyes never left those of the coloured man. 'Well, slave? Are you going to draw or will you take what's coming?'

Joe didn't move. He was no coward, but courage alone wasn't enough. In a straight gun-fight with this man he stood no chance. He was no longer young, he had spent the best part of his life as a house servant, and even the hardships of the past few months hadn't automatically given him the power of a lightning draw and a sure aim. That was why he carried a shotgun instead of a rifle. He wore a pistol only because without it he would have been treated little better than a dog.

'I don't want to fight you,' he said stiffly. 'I've no quarrel with you. Why don't you just forget it?'

'Forget it?' The man threw back his head and laughed. 'Hear that? He's got a yellow streak as wide as he's tall. A slimy yellow-belly, that's all he is. A dirty slave.' He stopped laughing and thrust his head forward. 'Slave,' he said deliberately. 'That's what you are. A dirty, yellow slave. That's right, ain't it?'

Joe didn't answer. The insults were nothing, he had borne far worse when he had been property and the young bucks had thought it funny to bait him. Then he had swallowed his anger and bowed his head, to do otherwise would have resulted in having the flesh whipped from his bones. Now, despite his knowledge that to reach for his gun would be simple suicide, he had to fight against the temptation to die like a man. The insults he could accept. Death itself he could willingly risk, but he had something to do and he didn't want to die before he had seen it done. And yet he was in an impossible position.

To back down would brand him a coward, make him the butt of every drunken white man in town and, knowing these men, Joe knew that they wouldn't stop at sheer horse-play. They would torment him beyond all reason, their sadistic fury mounting at his non-resistance, and in the end they would kill him. Joe knew that he wouldn't be the first man to by lynched or dipped in tar and ignited to run screaming, a living torch through the town while men jeered and laughed at his agony.

And Grant couldn't help him.

If he interfered then so would Bill's

friends, and it would be a gang against the two of them. Worse, as he and Grant had arrived together and were known to be companions, his cowardice would be that of his friend. Grant, no matter how much he wanted to protect Joe, could not do it and remain within the rough and ready code of the West.

'I'm waiting,' said Bill, and a thin trickle of saliva ran from the corner of his mouth. 'You're a dirty slave, ain't you? Say it, or draw!'

'You fancy yourself with a gun, don't you?' said Joe, and was surprised to find his voice so even. 'I wonder if you're man enough to stand up to a knife?'

'I'll bet that he isn't,' said Grant quickly before Bill could answer. 'I'll bet a hundred dollars that in a knife fight Joe here wins.' He looked at the ring of men surrounding the pair. 'How about it, fellas? Who'll cover me? A hundred dollars on Joe.'

'I'll take that,' said a new voice, and a man, white faced, white handed, dressed in a black broadcloth and looking every inch the professional gambler he was, nodded to the tall man.

'It's a bet,' said Grant quickly. 'If Joe wins then you pay me, if Bill wins then I pay you.' He sucked in a deep breath. 'Right, let's get on with it.'

'Hadn't you better ask Bill about that?' A short, red-headed man hitched at his belt and spat on the floor. 'I don't reckon he takes kindly to a stranger interfering in his business.'

'Of course, if Bill's afraid to meet Joe with a knife then we'll forget it,' said Grant casually. 'Seems to me, though, that a man who talks big should act big or shut up.' He smiled at the hate-distorted face of the crouching man. 'Surely you aren't afraid to meet a dirty slave with a knife, Bill, a big man like you.'

'Who are you to interfere?'

'Interested?' Grant sidled closer, hoping that the man would forget his quarrel with Joe and give him a chance to end the trouble. He smiled, still casual, but automatically he tensed, a slight tightening of his muscles, and Bill, wise in the way of gunfighters, recognized the signs.

He recognized something else too. He recognized the cold, almost feral light in the tall man's eyes and something, some residue of sense, warned him to avoid combat with the smiling stranger. He glared and spat and looked at the faces watching him.

'Well?' The gambler looked impatient. 'Do you back down or meet Joe here with a knife?'

'I ain't no knifer,' snarled Bill. 'Hell, when I fight I don't aim to mess about.'

'He's called you, Bill,' said the gambler casually. 'It don't take much of a man to gun a dirty slave. It don't even take much of a man to knife one. Seems to me that you talked out of turn.'

'Go to hell,' snapped Bill, but as he stared at the crowd around him he knew that he had lost their support. To them a fight, any fight, offered the promise of fun. They had been all ready to back up any play he might make against Joe and had thrilled with callous excitement to the thought of a man shot down in cold blood. Grant, by his interference, had offered them something new. His suggestion for matching the two men with knives had received immediate approval. No one seemed to remember that he had done it only to follow up Joe's own suggestion.

Bill knew that, knew too that if he backed down it would be he who would be branded the coward. Not that it would hurt him as it would Joe, his reputation was such that no man would dare to jeer at him, but despite that he would lose something, something which he, as a bully, prized above all else. Men would cease to fear him, and eventually one of them would challenge him and gun him down.

Like it or not he had to fight the way Joe wanted.

'I'll take him,' he snapped. 'I'll slit his black hide for him. Knives? I'll fight a dirty slave with anything he can name.'

Grant sighed and looked at Joe. How good Joe was with a knife Grant didn't know, but no matter what happened he had been saved from the blasting death of a gun duel in which he stood no chance.

The rest was up to him.

Joe himself felt nothing but relief. He had fought with knives before, back in the old days when the slaves had had their own quarrels and a knife was the only weapon they knew. They had been bitter, those fights, conducted in the firelit darkness of a slave hut, away from the sharp eyes of the overseers, when dark bodies had strained and fought while razor-edged steel had flashed and dulled as blood mingled with sweat on the slippery skins. Savage fights, merciless, fights stemming from hatred and rage and a desperate desire to escape from the animal lives they were subjected to.

Joe only hoped that his soft years as a servant had not robbed him of all skill.

He hoped still more when he saw

where Bill carried his knife.

The bearded man sneered as he prepared himself for battle. He hitched up his guns, wiped his hands on a soiled neck scarf, shuffled his feet and then, with deceptive slowness, lifted his right hand to the back of his neck.

It was a harmless gesture, the sort of thing any man might do, his hand lifting as if to scratch an offending itch before settling down to serious business. It fooled almost everyone in the crowd. It did not fool Joe.

He ducked and stepped aside as Bill's right hand, now moving with incredible speed, swept down from his collar carrying the knife he had concealed in a sheath fastened to his shirt. Even as he stepped aside, Joe's hand flashed to his own blade and after the first quick flurry the two men faced each other, each gripping a wickedly-curved knife, their left hands extended, their eyes wide, their breath whistling through their nostrils. Dust rose from beneath their heavy boots as they circled for an advantageous position, and as they moved the crowd surged back to give them room.

'Want to double the bet?'

Grant turned as a voice spoke at his side and he recognized the gambler.

'I didn't know Bill hefted a blade in his collar,' said the gambler casually. 'I reckon a man who does that knows his business. Want to double?'

'I'll double.' Grant stared towards the circling men.

Bill was growing impatient. He wanted to close in, drive home his knife, get the thing over with. Like most bullies he had a secret fear of cold steel. To squeeze a trigger was one thing, to face a man armed equally well was another. A pistol he could have faced, secure and confident in his own prowess, but a knife, wielded by an unknown, was something else.

He weaved, shifted and slashed at Joe as he stepped forward. Joe grunted, dodged away from the razor-edged steel, and felt his shirt gape as the knife grazed his side. Immediately Joe attacked, throwing the stiffened fingers of his left hand towards Bill's eyes, then as the man jerked his head away from the threat to his eyes, moved forward. He didn't slash, but drove the blade, edge upwards, in a ripping thrust towards the other's stomach. Had the blow gone home it would have disembowelled him and the fight would have been over. Almost it went home, but something, some instinct, caused Bill to throw himself backwards so that the point of the knife missed its target and instead of sinking into flesh merely ripped his shirt from waist to throat.

The crowd sighed and Bill kicked Joe in the shin.

Joe staggered, numbed and shocked with pain, and before he could recover Bill was advancing, again using his knife to slash and cut, the trick of a man who knows how to use a knife. A thrust, to a knife fighter, is something to be avoided. If it strikes home it is a one-shot chance. The blade could stick in a bone, miss, be torn from a hand. Also once driven home it is useless as a weapon of defence. A slash, on the other hand, can cause gaping wounds, sever tendons, cause weakness by loss of blood and carelessness due to pain. Only when the opponent has been rendered helpless does the experienced knife fighter move in for the killing thrust.

Sparks flew from the knives as Joe parried the vicious slash to his chest. His left hand darted out, grabbed Bill's knife wrist, slipped, then returned to knock it aside. Again he thrust and again he missed, then the crowd gasped as a line of blood appeared on the black skin. Bill grinned when he saw it, weaved, parried another thrust, stepped forward, his own blade sweeping in a cutting arc, then screamed as steel slashed across his right forearm.

'My man wins,' said Grant emotionlessly as Bill's knife fell from his nerveless hand.

'He wins,' admitted the gambler. He sucked in his breath. 'Man, but that was neat. A thrust as a feint, a parry and a return slash to cut the tendons and disarm.' He stared at Grant. 'Joe, whoever he is, is no novice.'

'He's fought before,' said Grant casually, then tensed as he saw Bill.

The defeated man was insane with pain and terror. Pain from the burning cut across his forearm which had crippled him, terror at the knowledge that from now on he would be crippled in his right arm. The tendons had been cut, and tendons do not heal. His right arm would remain stiff and awkward for the rest of his life.

Bill was a gunfighter, a man who depended on his skill and speed of draw. He was right-handed and, as he thought of what had been done to him, he went kill-crazy with hate.

'You slimy bastard,' he grated. 'You've crippled me, you scum! Hell, you're going to pay for this!'

His left hand moved from where it

gripped the gaping cut on his right arm. It lowered to the holstered pistol at his waist. His fingers curled about the butt, lifted the weapon, his thumb cocking back the hammer as his finger tightened around the trigger. It was fast, very fast, but to Joe the whole episode seemed to be taking place in slow motion.

He stood before the bar, staring at the man he had beaten in fair fight, and watched as death grinned at him from the orifice of the pistol. He felt disinterested, almost unaware of any sense of urgency and was not conscious of doing anything to save himself.

He forgot the knife he still held in his hand. He made no conscious gesture and wasn't aware of what he had done until he saw the end results.

Then he saw something suddenly sprout like an ugly growth on the throat of the man before him.

Bill swayed, his eyes surprised, the gun in his left hand suddenly too heavy to hold. He spun and slowly, from the knees up, twisted and fell into an untidy heap, the hilt of the thrown knife rapping against the boards of the floor as he rolled.

'Neat,' said the man with the red hair. 'Fastest throw I ever saw.' He stared down at the dead man. 'I guess you won, Joe.'

'With a knife,' said Joe. 'I fought him with a knife.'

'Sure,' said the red-haired man casually. 'It was a fair fight. I guess you just called his bluff.' He stirred the dead man with his foot. 'Want your knife back?'

'Yes.' Joe stooped, tugged, wiped the crimson blade on the dead man's shirt and tucked it back into its sheath. His hands were trembling with reaction and he stood wondering what was going to happen next.

Nothing did. The crowd dispersed, a couple of men nodded to him with friendly expressions, the piano struck up a jangling tune, and the fat bartender, sweating and more greasy than ever, vanished to reappear with a couple of youths. They picked up the body, took it outside, and the Mexican sprinkled sawdust over the stains.

Joe turned as Grant touched him on the shoulder.

'You won two hundred dollars,' he said easily. 'This man covered my bet.'

'It was worth it,' said the gambler. He looked distastefully at the sawdust. 'Hell, let's all have a drink.'

4

The gambler's name was Dan Holden and he was a strange combination of culture and brutality. He ordered a bottle of tequila, led the two friends to an empty table in a corner of the big room, poured liberal portions of the spirit. He passed around the drinks, lifted his own glass, and looked at Joe.

'A toast,' he said. 'To Joe, here, and a good day's work.'

'I take it that you don't mourn the passing of our late friend,' said Grant drily. 'Seeing as how he lost you a couple of hundred dollars, maybe you've got reason.'

'Bill was a rat,' said Holden easily. 'A gunfighter who was getting too big for his boots. That sort never lasts long, but until the man big enough to cut them down comes along they can make life pretty unpleasant.'

'If he made life so unpleasant, then why didn't someone call him before?' Grant sipped his drink and put down the almost untouched glass. He, like Joe, had learned to hold the raw liquor sold in the taverns of the West, but he had ridden all day with little food and he wanted to keep his wits about him.

'Bill was a fast man with a gun,' said Holden. 'He could outdraw any man in Alamatri and all of us knew it. It was clever of you to swing things so that he'd have to fight with a knife.'

'I didn't swing anything,' protested Grant. Holden shrugged.

'No?'

'No.'

'My mistake,' said the gambler. 'When Joe challenged him you seemed quick to take it up and make a bet out of it. I covered you because I could see that, unless I did, the idea would have flopped. Even at that I thought Bill had a chance, it seems that Joe here knew what he was doing.'

'I knew,' said Joe, and then sat silent,

his dark eyes shifting watchfully over the crowd. He, as he had done for months now, was watching for a sign of any of the five men he was searching for.

'Anyway,' continued Holden, 'it's over and done with. Bill's in Boot Hill by now and the Mexicans are probably dicing for his gear. Forget him.' He leaned forward a little and lowered his voice. 'The point now is, what are you aiming to do?'

'Look around,' said Grant curtly.

'Sure, but at what?' Holden grinned and took a pack of cards from his vest pocket. He leaned back in his chair, his long, white fingers riffling the deck, but despite his seeming indifference, his eyes were intent.

'A couple of strangers drift into town,' he said quietly. 'Within ten minutes one of them has killed the town bully. You wonder why I'm curious?'

'Curious about what?'

'Where you come from. Where you're

going. What you aim to do.'

'You're asking a lot,' said Grant stiffly. He pushed away his glass. 'Talk's cheap, but those questions aren't the sort which can be answered by the price of a drink.'

'True enough,' admitted Holden, and the cards flashed from hand to hand as he manipulated the deck. 'Don't get me wrong, Grant. I'm not the law and I'm not curious. Maybe I can help you. I've lived in this town for almost a year now and there's little going on that I don't know about. You want to learn the ropes? Then I can steer you right.'

'I'm looking for someone,' said Grant slowly. 'A pard of mine. We got separated a few months ago after a rumpus in the Civil War. I'd hoped to meet up with him in these parts.'

'It's a big country,' said Holden enigmatically.

'Not that big.'

'Not for men in the same line of business,' agreed the gambler. He hesitated, looking at his cards then, as if

71

on sudden impulse, closed the deck and thrust them back into his pocket. 'I'm not asking,' he said tensely. 'And I'm not telling, but look at it this way. Up north lies Indian country. Up north lies gold mines and trading posts. They've even started up a stage route, the Butterfield Stage, and it runs right through Apache Pass. Tucson isn't too far away and the settlers from the East are passing through to California. There's gold in California, gold in Dakota, gold in Colorado. South of the border, where we are now, no one asks any questions. Do you begin to get the picture?'

'I think so.'

'A few men, tough, hard, ready to take chances and with good mounts could hit, clean up and run. Before anyone knew who they were or what they were doing they'd be safe across the Rio Grande. Gold, Grant, furs and gold and it wouldn't even be necessary to fight for them. Give a few braves a rifle, some ammunition, a skinful of rot-gut and sit back while they go on the warpath and collect the loot.' He leaned forward, his eyes eager. 'How does it sound?'

'Sounds like you're giving a man a good idea,' said Grant casually. 'Some men might even go ahead and try it.'

'On their own?' Holden smiled. 'Listen, how far do you think they'd get? I told you that up north is Indian country. The Indians don't like white men and they like Mexicans even less. Try to contact them and your scalp will decorate a wickiup. Try to travel through the country and you wouldn't last a day. Do you know how the Indians treat any prisoners they catch? They don't like white men, Grant, and they aren't gentle. Slow roasting over a fire is about the best that can happen. I don't even like to think about the worst.'

'Now you're talking me out of a good idea,' said Grant evenly. He looked at Joe. 'Maybe we'd better find a room for the night and get some food. I'm hungry.'

'You can eat later,' snapped Holden irritably. 'The hotel will fix you up.' He leaned forward again. 'Are you interested in a proposition?'

'No strings?'

'No.'

'Then I might be interested,' said Grant casually. He stared at the gambler. 'Don't get the wrong idea, Dan. We aren't a couple of saddle-tramps broke and desperate. We can get by on what we have, and when that's gone we can always get more. We're in no hurry.'

'You will be,' said Holden grimly. 'This town gets you, Grant. If you're wise you'll get out of here as fast as you can. The heat gets you, and the damn liquor, and the desert. I've seen men ride in here looking as if they owned the world and I've seen them after a while, broke, cadging drinks, finally stealing a horse and trying to get back through Indian country and civilization. Money goes fast when you've plenty to spend it on and nothing much else to do.'

'If it's as bad as that, then why do you stay?'

'You think I like it here?' Holden spat. 'I'm a gambling man and I keep solvent, but it's time I moved. I've taken too many suckers to feel safe and I've an itching between my shoulder blades. That's why I'm glad to see the end of Bill. He was getting a little too worried about losing his cash and getting a little too ready to do something about it.' He looked eager. 'Look, that proposition I mentioned — '

'You've been here a year, you say?' Grant shifted in his chair and looked over the crowd.

'That's right.'

'Many pass through town during that time?'

'Some, why?'

'I told you I was looking for a friend of mine. He would have maybe met a couple of other men. One of them was a fat man, a gambler like yourself, we called him Tiny. Know him?'

'Maybe.'

'Or a man named Kent?'

'A little guy?'

'Yes, he had a notched ear.' Grant chuckled. 'I was with him when he got it. Man! I've never heard such cursing! It did me good to hear it.'

'I can guess,' said Holden. 'Anyone else?'

'The Roper brothers, I rode with them a while and we didn't do too badly. There was another man, big, slashed down the left cheek.' Grant chuckled again. 'I'd sure like to meet up with Jud again.'

'Would you?' There was something in the gambler's voice which made Grant turn and stare at him.

'You sound as if you know him.'

'Maybe I do.' The gambler sat back, his eyes thoughtful. 'If you want to eat,' he said pointedly, 'don't let me stop you. I didn't know that you rode with *hombres* like Jud.'

'Don't let it worry you,' said Grant easily. He rose and jerked his head at Joe. 'Be seeing you, maybe.'

Holden nodded, he didn't seem anxious to follow up the suggestion.

Outside the tavern Joe looked at Grant and then, without speaking, the two men mounted their horses and rode to the livery stables. The barns were in back of the hotel, so called because it hired rooms and served food, and after seeing to the needs of their beasts folks took time to catch up on their own wants.

The food was greasy, over-spiced and badly cooked, but the two men ate it as though it were perfect. After wiping their plates they rolled cigarettes and, over a bottle of wine, discussed what they had learned.

'Holden knows the men we are looking for,' said Grant decisively. 'He knows Jud for certain and he doesn't like him.'

'Maybe we made a mistake in not listening to his proposition,' said Joe. 'We haven't much money and the sooner we earn more the better.' He stared down at the tip of his cigarette. 'I don't know about his suggestion, though. I don't want to murder anyone or set the Indians loose on the settlers.'

'That was talk,' snapped Grant. 'I think that Holden was trying us out, seeing how far we'd go and trying to get a line on us. I think that the man is desperate to get away, but for some reason he daren't try to make a run for it on his own. He might be trying to get us to join him to protect him on his journey.' He shrugged. 'Not that it matters. If he wants us he'll talk to us again.'

He sighed as he stared at the dirty wall of the room in which they sat. It was galling to know that someone could help them but, for reasons of his own, probably wouldn't. Holden could set them on the right trail, Grant was sure of it, but unless he could make the man trust him absolutely he doubted if the gambler would talk. His fear of Jud was too obvious, even though he had hidden under a mask of indifference and dislike. To win his confidence wasn't going to be easy.

'Let's get started on a different line,' said Grant suddenly. 'You walk around and question the Mexicans. You may be able to win their friendship easier than I. You know enough Spanish to understand what they say, and after your fight with Bill you'll be a bit of a hero. Unless I'm mistaken these Mexicans have little love for the white men. They tolerate them for the money they spend, but that's about all.'

'I'll do that,' said Joe. 'And you?'

'Even though there's no law in this place yet, there is a church. If there isn't there will be a mission or something like that. The Mexicans are strongly religious and wouldn't be without a padre. I'll find him, talk to him and see what I can find out. We'd better meet again in the tavern, it'll be getting dark soon and that's about the only safe place to wait at the moment. Bill might have had a couple of friends who thought enough of him to get their own back on the man who killed him, so be careful.'

'I'll be careful,' promised Joe. 'Very careful.' He crushed out the butt of his cigarette and left the room. After a while Grant followed his example.

It wasn't too hard to discover where the padre lived. A young girl stared at Grant with liquid eyes and sullenly pointed to an adobe house set at the edge of the town. The padre himself was an old, withered man, as different from the indolent Mexicans around him as Grant himself was to the renegade whites. He bowed as he saw Grant and led the way into a cool patio ringed with great jars of water and sweetly scented by the heady odour of potted blossoms.

A young boy, his face that of an angel, his left foot cruelly twisted and dragging after him as he walked, brought wine and water. Grant stared after him then, aware of the gentle eyes of the old man upon him, flushed and looked away.

'Benito is a gracious child,' said the

padre softly. 'He would play all day in the sun, and if he was naughty and disobedient at times, who could blame him for that? It is a lasting thing for wonderment that the Good God saw fit to give him a cross to bear which all men can see.'

'He wasn't born like that then?'

'No, my son.'

'An accident?'

'The will of God, my son,' said the old priest softly. 'The will of God and, perhaps, a drunken man with a pistol who gained amusement from making little Benito dance as the bullets dug into the sand at his feet.'

'I see.' Grant thinned his lips as he thought about it. He had seen crazed men acting that way before, shooting at a victim's feet so that he jumped and capered to escape the bullets. Benito hadn't been lucky, the gunman had been careless and one of the heavy slugs had smashed the tiny foot to everlasting ruin.

'It was the will of God,' repeated the

old priest gently. 'His mother wept, but the world is full of sorrow, and what is one small boy against the misery of the world? But Benito would have made a fine gaucho.'

'And the man who did it?'

'Gone, *señor*. Gone with the wind and the rain and the flowers which bloom only to fade in a single day.'

'I see,' said Grant again. He looked down at his hands and then, as the old priest poured wine, looked up, his decision made.

'I have come a long way, Father,' he said slowly. 'I too have been, even as Benito, the sport of men and things which had better not seen the light of day. You have heard of the Civil War?'

'The world has heard of it, my son. Brother against brother, family against family. War is a thing of horror and a hateful thing, but war between those of the same blood and the same tongue is the most frightful form of war there can be.'

'It is over now,' said Grant. 'It is over,

but many things were done and which now cannot be undone. Bad men did crimes of darkness and blood. Those men have, as yet, gone unpunished. I am looking for five such men.'

'And when you find them?'

'They will be punished.'

'By the law?'

'By me.'

'I understand.' The old padre bowed his head and his thin fingers toyed with the worn beads of the rosary around his waist. 'I guessed as much when you entered this room. You are an unhappy man, my son, a bitter man. You are alive but not alive, for you live for hate and hate is a destroyer. Get rid of the hatred in your heart, tear it out as you would tear a viper from your throat. Kill your hate, my son, or it will kill you.'

'The men of whom I speak,' said Grant tightly, 'killed and tortured those who gave me birth. They took what was offered in friendship, accepted the hospitality which was freely given, and in return they burned and destroyed. Is it right that such men should go unpunished?'

'They will be punished,' said the old priest with calm conviction. 'But who are you to set yourself above the law? You seek to find these men and when you have found them you will kill them.' He raised one thin hand at Grant's gesture. 'You will do that, I read it in your heart. You will kill and in so doing you will become as they are. For it is not for you to take life, not for any man. It is not for you to take vengeance. It is not for you to hate.'

'That is for me to decide,' said Grant. 'All I ask is for information, nothing else. You must know all who pass through Alamatri. I ask only that you tell me if you know of these men, how long they stayed, in which direction they went. This I ask, nothing more.'

'I cannot help you.'

'You can if you would.' Quickly Grant described the five men and his reasons for knowing that they must have passed through the town. The old priest heard him in silence, his eyes withdrawn, his fingers telling his beads as they had told them countless times in his long life. When Grant had finished he sat as motionless as though carved from wood, and it was only when Grant stood up that he moved.

'More wine, my son?'

'No.' Grant stared helplessly down at the priest. 'You weren't listening to me,' he accused. 'You closed your ears.'

'I cannot help you, my son. I did not listen, for the flesh is weak and perhaps you may have read something in my eyes. I cannot help you find your own destruction. It is wrong for any man to take unto himself the role of avenger. Forget these men and return to your home. Work and build that which has been lost and destroyed. Do not live in hate, my son, but in love and peace.'

'Is that all you have to say?'

'That is all.'

Grant sighed, hesitated, and then recognising the futility of argument turned and strode from the room. He had almost reached the thick, nail-studded outer door when he heard a voice call to him and, turning, saw the crippled Benito dragging his twisted foot in his haste to reach him.

'*Señor*,' gasped the boy. 'I listened as you spoke, it was sinful of me to do so and undoubtedly the good Father would be hurt if he knew, but I know of one you seek.'

'You do?' Grant stepped forward and caught the boy by the shoulder. 'Tell me.'

'The bad one with the scar, the man called Jud.' The boy almost spat the name and his angelic face twisted in anger. 'It was he who played with me and caused my mother to weep. It was he who ruined my foot and lost me the chance of becoming a gaucho.'

'Where is he now?'

'I do not know. The others of which you speak I did not see, only the big man with the scar. After I was hurt my friends went to look for him, but he had gone. His horse and many goods had also gone. It was said that he rode north.'

'Do you know where? Was a name mentioned, a town?'

'No, *señor*.'

'I see.' Grant stared thoughtfully at the smooth face of the cripple. 'You want me to find him?'

'*Si, señor* I want you to find him very much.'

'I can guess why,' said Grant. He dug into his pocket and pressed gold into the boy's hand. 'For your mother, little one, and perhaps she may spare a prayer for me.'

'She will say many prayers for you, *señor*,' said the boy fervently. 'And I too shall pray.'

'Thank you,' said Grant, and pushed open the heavy door. Behind him the cripple stared at the smooth, easy movements of the tall man, and as he stared his face twisted with anger.

'*Señor!*'

'Yes, Benito?'

'Remember what he did to me, *señor*.'

'I will remember.'

'He made me dance to the bullets from his guns, señor, remember that.'

'You want me to make him dance also, Benito?'

'No, señor, for the good Father would not like me to hold evil thoughts, but remember what he did to me.'

'Yes,' said Grant. 'I shall not forget.'

'Good luck, señor,' called the boy as the tall man strode away down the darkening street. 'I shall pray to all the Saints to guide you in your search.'

He fell silent as the tall man vanished from view, and as he closed the door, moving awkwardly on his crippled foot, his face was wet with tears of hate.

'And I shall pray to the Devil,' he hissed. 'He shall also remember and perhaps he will not forget.'

Then, because he was truly pious, he crossed himself.

5

The tavern was full when Grant walked in from the darkening street. Night had fallen with the swift, brief twilight over almost as soon as the sun had lowered itself beneath the horizon and, with the coming of darkness, Alamatri seemed to really come to life.

Behind the long bar the sweating Mexican, now assisted by two sullen-faced youngsters with pock-marked cheeks and the hilts of knives conspicuous at their waists, served an unending stream of liquor to the thirsty customers. The piano, covered in glasses and with a thin, anaemic-looking man pounding the worn keys, kept up a ceaseless jangling which was lost in the mounting din of coughs, scraping boots, loud voices, yells, demands for drinks and the shrill laughter of women as they passed from man to man. They were the hostesses whose one task was to make the customers spend as much in as short a time as possible, and from the yells and noise which followed them they seemed to be doing a good job.

Grant stared through the coiling clouds of cigar and cigarette smoke, his eyes narrowed as he looked for Joe. He relaxed as he saw the negro, a cigar between his lips and a foolish grin on his face, leaning at one end of the bar. He stood alone, a little island in the sea of jostling bodies, and Grant guessed that his elbow room was due to his newly-acquired reputation as a dangerous man to trifle with. He took the cigar from his mouth as Grant joined him, lost his foolish expression and became serious as he lowered his voice.

'Learn anything, Grant?'

'Jud was in town. He got drunk, shot a boy in the foot, then ran towards the north. That's all I could learn. And you?'

'The same and a little more.' Joe nodded to a man who thrust a drink towards him, waited until the man had vanished from sight, then threw the contents of the glass into the sawdust on the floor.

'They keep buying me drinks,' he explained. 'I don't know whether it is because they want to thank me for killing Bill or because they want to get me drunk so that they can kill me in revenge. But I'm taking no chances.'

'Keep to that,' said Grant tensely. 'What did you learn?'

'Jud was here and Tiny was with him. The fat man was here first and he and Holden had some sort of gentleman's agreement. I think that Kent must have passed through after Jud left. The people I spoke to knew the Ropers by reputation, but they either didn't know or wouldn't tell me if they had passed through Alamatri with the others.' Joe sighed. 'They must have used this place as a rendezvous point in case they ever became separated. As far as I could learn they must have left here at least three months ago.'

'That fits in.' Grant looked over the crowd and then stared thoughtfully to where Holden sat at a poker table. He looked as cool as a gambler should be, but Grant, wise in the little things which betray a man's tension, knew that the gambler was a mass of nerves. His eyes sharpened as he stared at the others playing against the gambler.

'Joe! That man to Holden's right. His left hand!'

Joe sucked in his breath. 'The tattoo!'

'Yes. You said that the Roper brothers had a tattoo on the back of their left hands. Was it the same?'

'I think — ' Joe grunted and moved through the crowd. He stood for a while staring at the poker players, and then as the tattooed man lifted his head, moved back towards Grant.

'Well?'

'I'm not sure. That man is wearing a beard and the Ropers were clean-shaven. The tattoo is the same, though, I'd swear to that.'

'It could be a coincidence,' said

Grant, and tried to calm the twitching of his muscles. 'That particular pattern could have been on many men.' He looked towards the poker game. 'I'm going to sit in and play, Joe. You stand by in case of trouble. If you're sure that you recognize that man as one of the Ropers, signal to me.'

'Will you kill him, Grant?'

'Just signal.'

Grant stepped forward, trying not to stare at the tattooed man, and stood over the poker table. Holden glanced up, then as he saw who it was, smiled.

'Grant! Good to see you. Sitting in on the game?'

'Want to lose more money?'

'I'll lose it if you can win it,' said the gambler evenly. 'Well?'

'What are the stakes?'

'Table stakes, sky's the limit. Want in?'

Grant nodded and sat down opposite the suspected man. He pulled a handful of gold pieces from his pocket, the double-eagles which he had won earlier in the day, and threw a coin into the ante. Holden dealt cards, the suspected man opened, Grant threw in his hand and watched as Holden won the pot.

'You're always winning,' snapped the man to Grant's right. He sat between Grant and the gambler and wore a checkered shirt which had long since faded in the sun. 'I've never seen such luck.'

'Pipe down, Lefty,' said the man to Grant's left. 'If you can't play then get up and sing a song.'

'Button your lip, Mike,' snapped Lefty. He looked at the suspected man. 'Mike's always talking too much, Sam, maybe we should do something about it?'

'Maybe.' Sam glowered at the cards he had picked up and tossed them towards the dealer. 'If you're going to shoot off your mouth, Lefty, then I quit. I'm aiming to play poker, not to swap gab.' He grinned at Holden, who sat between him and the man called Lefty. 'That's right, ain't it, Dan?'

'What's right?'

'It's Mike's deal.'

'Sure.' Holden smiled, but Grant could see the signs of mounting strain betraying themselves in the slight bunching of the muscles at the corners of his mouth, the lines at the corners of his eyes and the way in which his hands ever so slightly trembled as he touched his lips.

Holden was afraid.

Grant wondered why. His own excitement had died now that he knew the bearded man was one of those he had been seeking. It could be coincidence, but the name and the tattoo had settled it for him. He glanced up and stared at Joe.

Joe hesitated then slowly nodded his head.

Sam was the man.

He looked down again as Mike dealt out the pasteboards.

'Ante ten dollars,' he said. 'Jacks to open.'

'I pass,' said Sam.

'Pass,' said Holden.

'I'll open for ten,' grunted Lefty.

Grant nodded and threw a coin into the pot.

'I raise that double,' said Mike.

'I'll stay.' Sam threw twenty dollars towards the centre of the table, Holden followed his example, and Lefty, after looking at his cards, grunted and slid forward another ten dollars. Mike looked at Grant.

'And you?'

'I'll stay.'

'Discards.' Mike looked at his hand, threw out one card and picked up the rest of the pack. Sam tossed out three cards, Holden two, Lefty grinned and shook his head. Grant stared at his hand, four hearts and a club. He discarded the club.

'Bid twenty,' said Lefty.

Grant picked up the card Mike had dealt him and glanced at it. It was a diamond, he had failed to fill his flush, and he shook his head and tossed in his hand.

'Raise fifty,' said Mike.

'Out,' said Sam and scowled as he discarded his hand. Holden, as calm as ever, fingered a heap of gold and thrust it forward.

'I'll double your raise, Mike,' he said, and looked at Lefty.

'You don't scare me.' Lefty counted out a hundred dollars and thrust it forward, and then added another fifty.

'I'll stay and raise fifty.'

'Pat hand, uh?' Mike looked thoughtful. 'I guess what I hold is worth a little more. Raise her another fifty.'

Holden, his face expressionless, thrust forward a heap of coins.

'And fifty.'

'You guys are crazy,' said Lefty. 'Hell, I don't aim to be bluffed. I'll raise a round hundred!'

'Too high for me,' said Mike, and tossed in his hand.

'I'll just double that,' said Holden, and sat, his eyes alert as he watched the man at his side.

Lefty hesitated, licked his lips, then

scowled at the pile of gold in the centre of the table. The bidding and raising had been quick and there was now more than a thousand dollars resting on the green baize.

'I'll see you,' he snapped, and levelled the bets. 'Show your hand.'

Holden smiled and tipped his cards face upwards on to the table. Three kings and a pair of tens.

'A full house.'

'Hell!' Lefty swore as he threw down his cards. 'I had a pat hand, a straight, did you ever see such luck!' He turned and yelled to the bartender to send over a bottle of tequila. Holden, his features impassive, swept up the gold and picked up the cards.

'Your deal, Sam.'

'So it is.' The bearded man grinned at the gambler and dealt out the cards. Again Lefty opened, Grant and the others stayed, and the bidding commenced. This time the tall man had a better hand, three jacks, and he stayed with the bidding until his instinct warned him to throw in his hand. Sam and Holden seemed to have it between them, each raising the other a hundred dollars, and Lefty, gulping at his tequila, stared at the mounting pot with greedy eyes.

'I'll see you,' said Holden to Sam. 'What do you hold?'

'Two pairs.'

'You win.'

Without showing his cards the gambler threw them among the discards, swept the pack towards him, shuffled and poised them in his hand ready for dealing. Mike, after one bitter curse, fell silent, his eyes counting the gold the bearded man pulled towards him. Lefty spat, swore and reached for his bottle.

'Two pairs win? Hell! I threw in better than that.'

'Ante up,' said Holden coldly. 'Put up or shut up.'

Lefty swore again, but threw money into the pot. Grant followed suit, his eyes thoughtful, and as he picked up his cards he wondered what was going on.

No professional gambler would have let such a low hand win such a high pot. No man in such a game would have continued to bluff with only two pairs. Drunks and fools might think it clever to use the weight of their money to buy the pot but in such a game they wouldn't have stood a chance.

Grant glanced at his cards, then, his face impassive, opened the bidding.

'Open for ten.'

'I stay,' grunted Mike.

'Let's quit playing penny ante,' sneered Sam. 'I'll raise you fifty.'

'I'll stay,' said Holden quietly, and looked at Grant. Lefty, after one disgusted look at his cards had thrown them into the discard and was out of the game.

'I'll meet you and raise you the same,' said Grant evenly. He counted out a hundred dollars and pushed it to the centre of the table.

'Big time,' said Mike, and hesitated. 'Hell, how can I lose? I'll stay.'

'For how long,' sneered Sam. 'Make it another fifty.'

'I'll stay,' said Holden, and as he pushed forward a heap of coins his eyes met those of Grant. For a moment the two men stared at each other and though no word was spoken Grant had the impression that the gambler was desperately trying to give him a message.

Then the gambler looked away and the moment had passed.

'I'll stay,' said Grant coolly.

'Why not,' chuckled Mike, and he evened the betting. Holden nodded and picked up the cards ready to deal.

'Discards?'

Grant picked up his hand and glanced at it. Three aces, a king and a nine. He threw out the king and nine, tossing them face downwards into the centre of the table.

'Give me two.'

'I'll take one,' said Mike.

'The same for me,' grunted Sam.

Holden dealt out the cards, placed

two face down on the table, discarded a couple from his own hand and replaced them with those he had dealt. 'Bidding?'

'Fifty,' said Grant.

'I'll stay,' said Mike.

'Your fifty and a hundred more,' snapped Sam. He thrust forward money as though it were dirt. 'All right, gambling man, what now?'

'I'll come in for a hundred raise,' said Holden evenly.

Again his eyes met those of Grant. 'The more you put down the more you pick up.'

'That's right,' sniggered Sam. He glared at Grant. 'All right, tall guy, let's see the colour of your money.'

Grant hesitated. He carried all the money owned by him and Joe and he knew from bitter experience how easy it was to let good sense run away beneath the gambling fever. He had money, but after it was gone he didn't know where to find more. He picked up his cards, glanced at them and made up his mind.

'I'll raise another hundred.' He fumbled in his pockets, dragged out money and counted out three hundred dollars.

'I'm out,' said Mike disgustedly. 'You *hombres* can beat a straight, or if you can't then I'm a sidewinder.'

'A yellow sidewinder?' Sam grinned, his evil bearded lips parting in a sneer. 'Why don't you go and find yourself a greaser dice game? Seems to me that you're out of your class playing with real men.'

'You said?' Mike tensed, his hand dropping beneath the table to his side. Watching him, Grant knew that he was bluffing. Sam had no fear of the man, no friendship, either to talk to him as he had done. Mentally Grant chalked up the fact that, as far as he knew, Sam was alone in the tavern. Both Lefty and Mike were casual players unconnected with the bearded man.

'Beat it,' said Sam, scornfully. 'Reach for that hog-leg and I'll spill your marrow.' He grinned. 'Walk away, man, or get carried to Boot Hill. Well?'

He was dangerous, dangerous and just drunk enough to be in a fighting mood. Mike stared at the bearded man for a long second, gulped, reddened, then, rising, walked unsteadily away. Sam laughed.

'I knew he was yellow,' he sneered.

'Let's get on with the game,' said Grant. 'You want to stay?'

'Stay! Hell, man, I'm raising you another hundred.' Sam pushed forward a heap of coins. 'And you, Dan?'

'I quit.'

'You what?'

'I quit.' Holden tossed down his hand. 'You heard me the first time, Sam. I don't reckon my hand is good enough for a tough *hombre* like you.' He stared at the bearded man. 'Why, you getting anxious?'

'Me?' Sam laughed, but his eyes held an ugly glint. 'You're the one to worry, Dan, not me.' He glanced at Grant. 'You still playing?'

'Thanks for asking.' Grant felt in his

pockets. He was grateful to Holden for throwing in his hand when he did. Under the rules of poker a man had to put up or shut up, either meet the bidding or throw in his cards. If Holden had raised the bidding, if he had stayed in the game, Grant knew that he would have had to give up. He had little money left, only enough to meet Sam's last raise. He threw it into the pot.

'I'm seeing you.'

'Yeah?' Sam shrugged. 'What've you got?'

'Your ears bad?' Grant made no move to show his cards. 'I'm seeing you, turn 'em over.'

'Can you beat a flush?' Sam showed his cards with a satisfied smirk, one hand already reaching out to pull in the pot. Grant knocked it aside.

'Three aces and a pair of fives. A full house. I win.'

'You what!'

'I win.' Grant stared into the beady eyes and felt his anger rise within him, the burning anger for this man and what he had done and stood for. 'I win you dirty, yellow rattlesnake! Now take your paws off that pot before I knock them off!'

He was asking for trouble and he knew it but, even as the words left his lips, Grant knew that there was nothing else he could have done. It wasn't the thought of the money which concerned him. The pot consisted of more than two thousand dollars, a sizeable sum, but his hate of the man opposite to him made him forget what the wealth meant to Joe and himself.

'What did you say!' Sam stared at the tall man, his arm sweeping off the table, his eyes suddenly feral and gleaming above his beard. 'What did you call me?'

'Cut it out, Sam!' Holden, his white face beaded with perspiration, grabbed at the bearded man's arm. 'You were wrong in trying to grab the pot. Forget it.'

'Forget it!' Sam seemed almost beside himself with rage. 'You heard what he called me! Forget it! I'll forget it all right when this *hombre* is eating mud and not before.' He looked into Grant's eyes, his own glistening orbs flickering to where the tall man's hands rested in plain view. He smiled, a thin parting of his hidden lips, his shoulder tensed a little and his hand, the one which had swept from the table, crept towards the pistol at his side.

'Pull that iron and I'll blast you,' said Holden flatly. He stared at Sam, his eyes desperate in the white intensity of his face and his right hand rested beneath the lapel of his coat.

'Stay out of this, Dan,' snarled Sam. 'Pull that Derringer on me and you'll suffer for it. Don't get all worked up over this tall guy, it just ain't worth it.'

'No shooting in here, Sam,' said Holden again. 'There's no call for you to go kill-crazy. This is a fair game.'

'Sure.' Sam nodded, his eyes crafty. 'Just let this guy say he's sorry, that's all. Just let him relax and admit he was wrong. I'm not a hard man and maybe he's been drinking. Just let him pass me the pot and we'll forget it.'

Grant threw the cards into his face.

He hurled them with the full strength of his arm and the pasteboards, thrown as a solid unit, smashed against the bridge of Sam's nose with stunning force.

Sam yelled with rage and pain. He jerked to his feet and dabbed at his nose staring at the blood marking his hand. He swore, horribly, and his right hand darted for the pistol hanging low at his side.

He caught at nothing but empty air.

It staggered him. He grabbed again for the butt of the pistol which had always hung at his side and now had unaccountably vanished. He glanced down at the empty holster then, as he looked up, he blanched with fear.

'Don't kill him, Dan,' said Grant quickly. He looked from the tiny Derringer in the gambler's hand to where Joe, his black face impassive, stood just behind the trembling Sam, the captured pistol in his hand. Around them men, attracted by the sound of raised voices, fell away from the poker table at the prospect of flying bullets. From hard experience they knew that too often innocent bystanders sometimes became the target for wildly aimed lead.

'You can't kill me,' stammered Sam. 'I'm unarmed and it would be murder. You can't shoot me down like a dog.'

'No?' Grant stared at him and something in the tall man's eyes caused great beads of perspiration to stand out on the bearded man's forehead.

'Don't do it,' he screamed. 'Dan, don't let him do it!'

Grant took a slow step forward. His hands were still empty, the gun still hanging in its holster, but that fact gave Sam no courage. He had read what was in the tall man's eyes and he was terrified at what he had seen.

'Stop him, Dan! Stop him I tell you!'

'Why?' The gambler still held the Derringer but now it was held loosely, ready for immediate action if need be but without the threat of sure death.

'Jud'll hear about this,' said Sam. He recovered a little of his animal courage as nothing happened to him. 'Wait until Jud hears about this. You know what he'll do to you, Dan? He's learned a lot of tricks and by the time he's finished with you you'll be begging for a bullet. Stand by me, damn you, or you'll suffer for it.'

'Put away that Derringer, Dan,' said Grant evenly. He looked at the gambler as he hesitated. 'Put it away, man! Sharp!'

Holden obeyed the command in the other's voice.

'I'm not going to kill you, Sam,' gritted Grant tightly. 'That would he too easy. Instead . . . '

His fist smashed against Sam's injured nose.

It was a hard blow, a blow resulting from long months of brooding hate, and the force of it sent the other man staggering back against the wall. Before he could recover Grant was on him again, his fists pounding at the matted beard, the broken nose, the eyes, chin and throat. He struck and struck again at the man before him until suddenly he was striking against air and hands, many hands, were pulling him away.

'Stop it, Grant,' said Joe urgently. 'You'll beat him to death.'

Grant swayed and blinked the redness from his eyes.

'Yes,' he said slowly. 'Thank you, Joe. I don't want to kill him.' He straightened and rubbed the split knuckles of his right hand. 'Where's Holden?'

'Here.' The gambler moved forward, his face strained and anxious. Grant stared at him.

'You're in trouble, Dan,' he said evenly. 'I heard what Sam said and he's sure to tell Jud all about it. You're no friend of Jud and he's a bad man to cross.' He glanced down at the man at his feet. 'Seems to me that if you want to save your hide, you'd better start thinking.'

'You think I haven't already done that?' Holden shrugged. 'I made my play at the table, or didn't you catch on?'

'You let me win, I gathered that. Why?'

'You remember what I told you a while back. A proposition I had?'

'Yes?'

'It's still open. Interested?'

'No.'

'You want to find Jud, don't you?'

'Maybe.'

'That's not what I heard,' said Holden grimly. 'You've been asking questions around town. News travels fast in this country and how long will it be do you think before Jud gets word that two men are asking after him? Stay in Alamatri and you'll be bushwhacked for sure. If you want to stay healthy you've got to get out of town, head north, and I'm the man who can fix it for you.'

'Not on your terms.'

'Forget what I said a while back.'

Holden glanced at the men, still standing well clear, and lowered his voice. 'Look, I don't know who you are, you could be the law for all I care, but we need each other. I've got to get out of town and I've got to do it fast. I can't travel alone and, without me to guide you, you wouldn't get far. Travelling together we've got a good chance to make it across the border and through Indian country. Once north of the border and among our own people we'll be safe. Stay here and they'll be digging new graves in Boot Hill before you know it. Well?'

'Is Jud up north?'

'Yes. Is it a deal?'

Grant led the way outside.

6

It was night. From the north a thin wind carried the scent of sage and stirred the fine sand with invisible fingers as it lost itself towards the hills of the south. The moon had long set and the desert was lit only by the light of the stars, which, like a scattered handful of jewels, blazed from the bowl of the sky.

In the dim starlight the figures of three men with their horses showed as indistinct shadows against the rolling dunes of the desert.

'Are you sure he will come this way?' said Grant. He stooped and patted the neck of his horse then, as he had done for the past hour, turned and stared back along the way they had come.

'He will come,' said Holden grimly. 'I know Sam and I can guess what he will do. He'll never forgive you for what you did to him, me neither, and he'll want our blood.'

'He is a mean man,' said Joseph quietly. 'I've seen men like him before. Overseers and small owners who treated their slaves like dogs and worse than dogs. Sam is a bad man.' The negro shivered a little in the chill wind. 'I could do with some coffee.'

'No fires,' said Grant quickly. 'A fire can be seen for miles in the desert and we don't want him to know that we are here.'

'I can light a fire he won't see,' suggested Holden. 'An Indian scout taught me how to do it.'

'Did he tell you how to hide the smell of boiling coffee too?' Grant smiled towards the gambler, his teeth gleaming in the starlight. 'I remember once while out on patrol we caught a nest of Union Troops off guard. We did it by locating them by the smell of their coffee. They had a hidden fire too, but we left ten dead and took fifteen prisoners.' He chuckled softly as he thought about it.

'That was the dearest cup of coffee they had ever drunk.'

'Sam won't be able to smell no coffee,' said Holden. 'Not after what you did to his nose. If he can breathe at all through it it will be a miracle.' He slapped his shoulders. 'The desert gets cold at night, mighty cold. I reckon we've time for a cup of coffee before he gets here.'

Grant nodded, thinking about it. The gambler was right. The desert grew cold once the sun had set, the clear air did not retain much heat and, just as the sand grew too hot to touch during the day, so it grew cold after dark.

'If you're certain about the fire,' he said slowly. 'I guess that it wouldn't do much harm. I'd forgotten about Sam not being able to smell for a while yet.'

'He couldn't smell a livery stable,' chuckled the gambler. 'We'll be safe enough.'

He slipped from his horse and took kindling from his saddle-bags. He slipped his hunting knife from its sheath and whittled a heap of thin slivers of wood. Sparks flew as he scraped flint on steel and a little flame, dying almost as quickly as it rose, illuminated his face and hands with a ruby glow. Swiftly he scraped sand into a ring about the tiny blaze, fed it with kindling, set the coffee pot over the fire on a rough tripod, and then piled more fuel on the red glow.

Grant stared at it, biting his lip, then rode away from the fire back down the trail they had followed. He rode for fifty feet then turned and stared to where the fire must be. He saw nothing, not a glow, not a spurt of flame, just the starlit desert. He sniffed, his flaring nostrils catching a pungent, peculiarly familiar odour which grew stronger as he rejoined the gambler and Joe.

'Well?' said Holden. 'Was I right?'

'You can't see it,' admitted Grant. 'But you can sure smell it. What are you using for fuel?'

'The only fuel you can get around here. Dried droppings. Up north you can use buffalo chips, they burn sweet and clean, but down south we have to use what we can get.' He smiled as he tended the fire. 'I bet you recognized it.'

'Horse,' said Grant. 'And goat and cow.' He sniffed again. 'It smells like a farmyard.'

'It won't hurt you,' said the gambler. He tested the pot of coffee. 'I guess you ate worse and drank worse during the war'.

'Yes.'

'You too?' Holden glanced towards Joe where he sat, still on his horse, staring down the trail. 'You hear me, Joe?'

'I'm watching,' said Joe curtly. 'Listening too.'

'Leave him,' said Grant. He dismounted and joined the gambler by the fire. 'You haven't said much since we rode out of town, Dan. Maybe we should have a little talk.'

'About what?'

'You and us and Sam and the rest of the boys. What made you so eager to get out of town? The way Sam spoke I thought you was a friend of his.'

'Was is right. We ain't particularly friendly right now.' Holden sucked at his teeth. 'Come to think of it, there isn't much I know about you two either. Nothing, that is, except that you aren't all that friendly with a man called Jud.'

'That's right.' Grant paused, staring at the fire. They had left town in a hurry after he had beaten Sam, the gambler following them without question, and Grant had let the gambler more or less lead the way. He had led them to this spot and halted and now Grant felt it time for a showdown. He said so and Holden shrugged.

'We could have stayed around town and Sam would have tried to kill us all. He couldn't do it and he would have known it, but Sam isn't alone. He rides with and for a tough bunch and they would have come after us and flayed us alive. Me and you and Joe. All of us. Worse, there are plenty of men in

Alamatri who would have stepped in to help Sam. We wouldn't have stood a chance. I thought you knew all that when you took off the way you did.'

'I thought of more than that,' said Grant tightly. 'You still talking?'

'Why not?' Holden shrugged. 'My story's soon told. I drifted to Alamatri from the river boats, I had some idea of heading West and finally arriving in California. The Indian wars put a stop to that and so I had to turn south across the border. I met up with Jud and his boys there and we made a deal. I was to arrange shipments of guns and rot-gut and he was to pay for them with gold and skins. We made a couple of deals and then I got wise. Jud was using me, getting me in so deep that I couldn't back out.'

'Did you want to?'

'At first, no. It looked like easy money and, at that time, there was plenty of war surplus around. Guns were going begging, still are, from the manufacturers who are stuck with them now that the Civil War is over. They are eager to sell them to anyone with cash and they aren't too keen on asking questions. So they sell them to an agent in Mexico and they don't worry about what happens to them after that. You begin to get the picture?'

'Yes. Guns for the Indians. Guns to use against the settlers and the cavalry. Nice business.'

'So I'm no saint,' said Holden. 'Are you?'

'Maybe not, but arming the Indians is one thing I wouldn't do. I've seen too much war to want to curse the West with more of it.' Grant was surprised to find himself trembling. He stared at the fire and tried not to think about it.

'I said that I was no saint,' said Holden slowly. 'I'm a gambling man, always have been, and I'm ready to take a chance with the next man. Would you believe me if I told you that I had some crazy idea of helping the Indians?'

'Helping them? Against what?'

'Against us, the white man.' Holden

prodded at the fire and a puff of flame illuminated his features. Grant stared at him, seeing, for a moment, the real man beneath the facade of the professional gambler.

'Do they need help, Dan?' asked Grant quietly. 'And if they do, are you helping them by letting them kill our own kind?'

'The Indians are a great people, Grant,' said the gambler. 'I know. I've lived with them. I told you I drifted from the river boats and headed West. I fell sick, some sort of fever, and had to fall out of the wagon train. The Indians were peaceful then and after I recovered a little I took to trading with them. Mirrors, tobacco, beads and stuff like that for skins and what gold they had managed to pick up. They didn't think much of gold, Grant, they still don't think much of it. To them it's just a soft, yellow stone, useless for anything and they laugh at us for wanting it.' He shrugged and prodded at the fire again. 'So I traded with them and got to know them real well. More than well, in fact, they even took me into the tribe as a brother. I was with the Apaches, you know, the Arapahoes. I was with them when some drunken fool of an officer broke the treaty and set the West aflame.'

'So you tried to help them,' said Grant quietly. 'What then?'

'I wasn't an Indian,' said Holden curtly. 'I found that out. I was still a white man, deep inside of me where it mattered. I couldn't face it. I had to get out.'

'Yes?'

'Yes.' Holden turned and stared Grant full in the eyes. 'You've seen Civil War, Grant, you know what it's like. There's nothing so bad as a war like that. I was a white man living with the Indians and my people and they were at war. I couldn't face it. The Indians accepted me for what I was but my own people called me a renegade and an Indian-lover and tried to string me up when I called in for supplies. I was lucky to escape with my life.'

'So you rode south, across the border, and from here you shipped rifles up north.' Grant nodded. 'Where does Jud come in?'

'He had a guide, a half-breed Mexican Indian, who was related to one of the tribes. He fixed the deal. Gold for guns, he got the gold and I got the guns, simple.'

'Yes,' said Grant. 'Too simple. Why the change of heart?'

'Jud is rotten,' snapped Holden. 'He found out where the Indians find their gold, in one of their sacred burial grounds. That was enough for Jud. Now he wants to exterminate the Indians so that he can stake a claim to their gold and get rich. So he supplies them with guns and rot-gut whisky. He gets the young braves raging drunk and sends them out on the war-path. They kill a few settlers and the cavalry rides after them. In retaliation the cavalry destroys the Indian villages and decimates the tribe. They have a war, a real fighting war, and then a new treaty is fixed up. That lasts until Jud or someone like him breaks it again.'

'Same result,' said Grant quietly. 'Different motive. How are you better than Jud?'

'I thought that if I could give the Indians the power to defend themselves the white men would think twice before robbing them of the land the Indians have called their own for centuries. I thought that with guns they could kill more game and have time to try and learn the ways of the invader. Can you see that?'

'I can see it,' said Grant. 'But I can't believe in it. The Indian is finished, Dan. There aren't enough of them to hold back the settling of the West. They just can't keep their culture while all around them surges a new culture. They can't fight against the white men, Dan, if they do that they will be exterminated. To live at all they must learn to adapt. Giving them guns isn't going to help them. They will kill a few settlers but, in return, they will be killed. We can afford to lose a few thousand people. Can they?'

'No,' admitted Holden. 'They can't.'

He reached forward and touched the coffee pot.

'Ready yet?'

'Almost.'

'Good.' Grant warmed his hands at the dully glowing fire. 'So you had a working agreement with Jud and later regretted it. I suppose Sam was the contact man. Did he ride in to pay you?'

'Yes.'

'What went wrong?'

'Jud is after making a killing. He stored the guns up north somewhere and intends taking them up in one load. My guess is that he's contacted the Indians and wants them to collect. Or he might be playing a double game, getting what he can from the Indians, and then selling the guns to the settlers. That doesn't matter. I was supposed to have a new shipment waiting for him but I hadn't. Sam acted suspiciously the last time I saw him and I guessed that Jud was ready to eliminate me from the scene. For one thing he wouldn't have to pay a dead man and, for another, dead men can't talk. That's why I backed your play again Sam.'

'You fixed the cards so that we would quarrel,' said Grant. 'I know that. You also want help against Jud and you figured that we could help save your hide. Right?'

'Right.'

'It makes sense,' said Grant. 'And it all fits in. I beat up Sam and we ride out of town. Sam will recover and look for us. If he doesn't find us or if he wants some help he will ride to meet up with Jud. We stay on the trail until he passes and then we follow him. With any luck at all he will take us through Indian country to the hide-out where Jud is staying.' He looked at the gambler. 'That suits me fine, Dan, but what about you? Why can't you just head East and keep riding?'

'I don't like to be crossed,' said the gambler. 'And I want to live without the fear of a hand on my shoulder any moment. Jud's mean and he'll tip off the law about me. If he doesn't do that he'll ride after me himself. I don't want to live like that.' He licked his lips. 'But more important is that I've been doing some thinking. Maybe I'm beginning to think as you do or maybe I don't like the idea of Jud using the Indians for his own ends. The reason doesn't matter, but I'd be happier if those guns never reached Indian hands.'

He reached out and lifted down the coffee pot. He kicked sand over the fire until it was extinguished. He poured three cups full of the fragrant coffee, added a little whisky to each cup, and called to the silent figure of Joe.

'Hey, Joe! Come and get it.'

Joe didn't move.

'Step down and sit, Joe,' ordered Grant. 'We'll be able to hear a horse long before we can see it. Come over here and warm yourself.'

He waited until Joe had dismounted and was sitting between them sipping his laced coffee.

'You think that Sam will lead us straight to Jud?'

'Yes.'

'How will we follow him in the dark?'

'We won't,' said Holden grimly. 'I've given this some thought, Grant, and here's the plan. We trail Sam as far as we can and then we close up with him. He'll guide us through the foothills to the hide-out.'

'Will he?' Grant sounded dubious. 'Without him knowing it?'

'That's the idea.'

'It's a slim chance,' said Joe, suddenly. 'A man can see for miles in this country.'

'But not further on,' said Holden. 'The country breaks up over the border and the hills start. That's rough ground and we should be able to stay under cover.' He hesitated. 'If he does spot us we'll just have to ride up and grab him.'

'Wait a minute!' Grant frowned. 'You told us that a white man wouldn't stand a chance in Indian country. What makes us so special?'

'Me.' The gambler smiled as he sipped at his cup. 'I told you that I was accepted by the tribe. As far as they are concerned I'm still a member. I can get you through.' He drank more coffee. 'One thing, Grant . . . '

'Yes?'

'What makes you so eager to catch up with Jud and his boys?'

'Personal reasons.'

'So?' Holden shrugged. 'Put it this way, then: What do you aim to do when you catch up with them?'

'Kill them.'

'Kill . . . ' Holden drained his cup and nodded as a man would nod who has had a suspicion confirmed. He was about to say something when Joe, his face tense, lifted a hand for silence.

He listened, then, abruptly, rested his ear against the ground. When he straightened again he spoke in a low, tense voice.

'A horse! One horse riding fast towards us.'

It could only be Sam.

7

Sam rode with a total disregard for anything but the utmost speed. Savagely he spurred his horse, raking the heaving flanks with the sharp rowels until blood mingled with the sweat and dust. He needed no light to guide him, he knew the trail as well as he knew the contours of his own face, and so he rode with a loose rein cursing the jolting motion which brought fresh discomfort to his aching face and body.

His nose was broken, he knew that, and several teeth were missing from his gums. His stomach and chest seemed to be one bruise and his jaw was swollen and sore. But worse than his physical injuries was the hurt to his pride. He had ridden into town to kill Holden, shoot him down at his own pleasure and time and, while playing at poker, he had been anticipating the final climax of his errand. The tall stranger had upset those plans, the coloured man had rendered him helpless and then Holden, the man whom Jud had used and now wanted eliminated, had made him look a fool.

The three of them had to die.

He grinned as he thought about it. The Mexican bartender had thrown water into his face and given him a pistol. Sam had raged through Alamatri, a gang of scum at his heels, ready to lynch the three men if he had found them. From the livery stable he had learned that they had left town and, for a little while, Sam had trembled on the edge of forgetting his business to ride after them and hunt them down. His own fear of Jud, and the realization that it would be almost impossible to locate them in the dark, had made him cautious. Now he was riding back to the big man to tell him the news and to warn him that Holden had escaped.

That done, he would have all the time and help he needed to hunt down the man who knew too much. And when he found him Sam knew that he would also find the others with him.

The horse stumbled and Sam cursed as his broken nose throbbed with a sharper pain. He swore, quirting his mount, and dragging at the reins. The horse stumbled again and Sam, impatient as he was, knew that he must rest the horse or have it die beneath him.

Reluctantly he drew rein and looked about for a place to camp. It was almost dawn, the first faint light of the rising sun faded the stars and painted the east with pink and gold, red and orange. Around him the desert seemed almost unreal, a rolling expanse of dune and scrub with the dim shape of the hills rising before him to the north. Between him and those hills was the river, the border he must cross, and he was Westerner enough to know that without his horse he couldn't possibly accomplish his journey.

Again he stared about him, towards

the hills before him and the desert at each side.

He didn't look behind him.

Camp was a rough affair of a fire, coffee, bacon and beans, feed and water for the horse. While the coffee was boiling Sam rubbed down his mount and, after he had gulped his meal, relaxed, a rolled cigarette between his puffed lips, a thin coil of smoke rising into the windless air. He rested for an hour and then, flinging his saddle over the rested horse, remounted and continued his journey.

Three hours' fast riding brought him to the edge of the river and, without hesitation, he forced his horse to plunge into the wide, yellow stream. The current, though strong, was not fast and, without any trouble the horse mounted the far bank and stepped over the stones towards the foothills.

Sam rode more slowly now, his eyes alert and, after a few miles slowed down to almost a walk. He looked about him and grunted as he saw a patch of scrub to one side.

He drew rein, dismounted, and unsaddled his mount. Hobbling the horse he built a fire and, while it was catching hold, carefully stripped and cleaned both his rifle and pistol. He reloaded carefully, examining each cartridge before slipping it into the weapons, tested the firing pins and spun the chamber of his revolver. Satisfied with the condition of his arms he threw a double handful of wet grass on to the fire. Immediately a thick column of smoke plumed upwards into the air, a column which Sam broke into irregular clouds by covering the fire with his saddle blanket, trapping the smoke and then releasing it in a swollen cloud. He kept this up for five minutes and then, stamping on the fire, put it out. He saddled his horse, hitched his gun belt around his waist, and sat down between two rocks. Into his retreat he took his rifle and, almost hidden, he sat and waited while the sun grew hotter and hotter on his bruised features.

The half-breed arrived so quietly that Sam almost shot him before he knew who he was.

'You fool,' he called. 'I almost took you for an Apache. What kept you?'

'Many Indians,' said the half-breed. He was a squat, dirty, villainous old man, his skin so weathered and wrinkled as to resemble a monkey rather than a man. He was dressed in filthy skins and a shapeless hat. He squinted at Sam and waited until the white man had mounted and was ready to travel.

'We go fast,' he said. 'Many Indians with sharp eyes. They see smoke and come fast. We go before they come.'

'Sure,' said Sam. 'Let's go.'

The half-breed did not move.

'What's keeping you, Pedro?' Sam glowered down at the man from his saddle. 'If there are Indians around here let's move. I don't aim to swap no talk with Indians.'

'You pay,' said the half-breed and held out one dirty hand. 'You pay or we no go. I go, you stay.'

'Pay!' Sam. swore and cursed the guide in two languages. 'You've been paid. Jud paid you. You've got all the gold you're going to get.'

'No. Some gold, yes, but I want more, much more. The big man Jud, he promised me much gold but gave me little. Now you pay me or I go.'

'That's what you think,' said Sam grimly. His right hand moved and his pistol leapt into his hand. The hammer made a faint clicking sound as he drew it back with his thumb. 'Now, Pedro, let's get out of here. Try anything smart and I'll drop you. Move.'

'You kill me and the Indians kill you,' said the guide impassively. He stared at the muzzle of the weapon centred on his body. 'You give me gold now and I take you along trail to Indians. You choose.'

'You dirty old thieving varmint,' snarled Sam bitterly. 'I've a mind to plug you and take my chances.'

'Many Indians,' said the half-breed

evenly. 'They find you, they kill you — slowly.'

He was right and Sam knew it. The Indians were restless and the hills were alive with their scouts. The half-breed knew the trails, the paths which would lead to the hide-out and safety. Sam could kill him and try to make it on his own. He knew the general run of the hills and he could find the hide-out if he had to, but whether he could make it without being spotted by the Indians was another matter.

Probably they wouldn't kill him. The chances were high that he could talk fast and make a deal for, in a way, he had what they wanted. But if he saved his skin by betraying the whereabouts of the guns Jud would flay him and hang him on a cactus in the sun. If he remained loyal to the big man then the Indians would treat him as they treated all white men who fell into their power. Either way he couldn't win.

'You pay,' repeated Pedro evenly. 'You pay now, quick, before the Indians

139

come. You pay and we go.'

'I'll pay,' said Sam savagely. 'I'll pay, blast you, but we'll see what Jud has to say about this.'

He uncocked his pistol and thrust it into its holster. From a pocket he drew a handful of gold and threw it towards the half-breed. Pedro stooped, clawing at the bright metal coins, and, as he rose, he hid them among his rags. Silently he led the way into the scrub.

His horse was waiting a few hundred yards down the trail and Sam waited while the guide mounted. Together, the half-breed leading, they plunged into a maze of criss-crossing trails, wending their way between huge rocks and jutting outcrops. As they rode they began to climb higher and higher towards the hills and, far below them, the river sparkled as it wended its way across the horizon.

'This isn't the right direction,' said Sam after about three hours of progress. 'We're heading too far west.'

'Indian party about here,' said Pedro

shortly. 'We circle around them.'

'Yeah?' Sam turned in his saddle and squinted about him. 'You certain?'

'Yes.'

'You wouldn't have the idea of maybe leading me off the trail and then bouncing a rock off my head, would you?' Sam glared at the guide, his little eyes narrowed with suspicion. 'You know what the score is, Pedro. Play along with us and you'll get rich. Try anything smart and you'll wind up dead. If Jud don't get you my brother will. Don't forget that.'

'Indians on war-path,' said the guide stolidly. 'We miss them this way. We ride among them the other way. You want that you ride alone?'

'I don't want that,' snapped Sam irritably. His bruises hurt and he wanted a drink. Long hours in the saddle had made him tired and, even though he was still burning for revenge, the first fine edge of his impatient anger had worn away. Also — he was afraid.

He would never admit it, not even to

himself, but he was afraid of the Indians. He had seen them, tall, stern-faced warriors, and despite their primitiveness and lack of civilized culture he had known them for the better men. They terrified him with their cold ruthlessness, so different to his own hot anger, and once he had seen what they had left of a trader who had ignored all warnings and had robbed them. That man had died, not quickly, and Sam couldn't stop thinking about it.

At first he had been all for this deal with the rifles. Jud had talked them into it with promises of riches and unlimited gold. On the surface it seemed simple. Sell the guns to the Indians for all the gold they could manage to obtain. Then sell the ammunition for more. Never mind the bloodshed and killing which would result from the armed Indians attacking the wagon trains, the settlements and forts. Never mind the reprisals which would inevitably follow. To Jud the Indians were little more than wild animals, savages, hardly even worth calling human. He considered them only as a means for getting rich.

But Sam was thinking about the other side. The cavalry and white men wouldn't think highly of renegades who sold rifles to the Indians. They would hunt down the men who had done it and lynch them without trial or question. To be able to live long enough to enjoy their wealth Jud and his gang would have to play things very carefully indeed. That was why Sam had been sent to kill Holden. The gambler knew too much and was better dead.

What Sam didn't realize was that what applied to the gambler applied to the others too. Himself for one.

Pedro halted and slid from his horse.

'We camp here,' he said. 'Eat, rest horses.'

'Why?' Sam remained in his saddle, staring down at the half-breed. 'We don't want to waste time. Let's push on.'

'We camp,' repeated the guide evenly. 'We rest and then ride some more. Tonight, when the moon has set, we shall be on trail for hide-out. Now we eat.'

Sam cursed but dismounted. He had ridden hard and far and could do with the rest and his horse could do with it even more. The jaded beast gulped at the water the guide gave him and then moved to stand in the shadow of a boulder. Sam, after taking food and fuel from his saddle-bags, joined the guide where he sat building a fire between two stones.

'You reckon it's safe to build a fire?'

'No smoke from this fire,' grunted the half-breed. 'We boil coffee and eat. After we eat we ride hard so as to be on trail when dark.'

'How about the Indians?'

'Not here.' The half-breed pointed towards the horizon. 'See?'

Sam stared in the direction indicated

by the guide and sucked in his breath. Thin against the burning sky a thread of smoke lifted towards the heavens. It rose without break, a slender column of white almost motionless in the windless air.

'Smoke signal!' Sam glared at the guide. 'What does it say?'

'Nothing. Smoke means for Indians to attend parley. Peaceful signal.'

'You hope,' said Sam. He grunted as he sat down and touched his injured nose. It had swollen and now felt numb, the initial pain having died to a deep throbbing. The pain made him think of Holden and the tall man and he gritted his teeth with anger.

Pedro stared back down the way they had come, stiffened, then turned back to his cooking. Slight as the motion had been Sam had spotted it and, alert for danger, he rose and stared over the foothills.

'You saw something,' he snapped to the guide. 'What was it, Indians?'

'No.'

'What then?'

'Nothing.'

'You're lying, damn you!' Anger and fear made Sam even more irritable than before. He gripped the guide by the shoulder and spun him away from the fire. Pedro fell, twisting as he landed and his hand, moving with deceptive speed, flashed to his collar and down again. He halted the gesture, the knife he had drawn from its scabbard still poised for the throw.

'Drop it,' said Sam. He grinned down at the half-breed, the pistol in his hand a glinting finger of menace. 'Drop it or I'll blast you.'

Pedro dropped the knife.

'That's better.' Sam stepped forward and kicked the knife away from the crouching man. 'Never yet seen a greaser that I couldn't outdraw or outride. Now, what was it you saw back there?'

'Nothing.'

'Try again.' Sam squeezed the trigger of his pistol, his thumb holding back

146

the hammer and, slowly, he began to release it. Pedro licked his lips at imminent death.

'Nothing, *señor*,' he gasped. 'Men, white men, but they mean nothing.'

'White men!' Sam holstered his pistol with a gasp of relief. 'Is that all? How many?'

'Two, maybe three, no more.'

'When did you see them first?'

'Just now. Once before when they crossed the river. I . . . '

'They crossed the river!' Sam turned and glared back the way they had come. 'Three men you say? Was one of them coloured?'

'I do not know.' Pedro, moving with snake-like grace, recovered his knife and slipped it into its sheath. 'They mean nothing.'

'You fool!' Sam swore as he realized what had happened. 'They're following me, you dumb half breed. They are tracking us to the hide-out. Why didn't you tell me this before?'

'I did not know they were following

us,' said Pedro sullenly. 'I saw them cross the river, but what of that? Many men cross the river and why not? Then I did not see them again until just now. It was but a glance, no more.'

'But they are the same men who crossed the river?'

'I think, yes.'

'It's them,' said Sam, and his battered face twisted into a smile. 'Good. Now that I know they're here I'll be ready for them.' He stared about him and snapped his fingers. 'A trap. Listen, Pedro, those men are after our scalps. If they catch up with us we'll be cut down for sure. We've got to blast them first.' He crossed to his horse and took the Winchester from its scabbard.

'You keep cooking, make plenty of noise and talk to yourself so as to make out that we are together. I'm going to move away a piece and surprise them as they get close. When you hear the shooting duck out and circle to take them from the rear. You get that?'

'You pay me?'

'Sure I'll pay you.' Sam chuckled. 'You can have what we find on them after they are dead. I know for sure that they are carrying plenty of dinero. It's all yours, Pedro, just as soon as you can take it from them.'

'Much gold?' said Pedro, his eyes were shining.

'Much gold,' chuckled Sam. He had recovered his good humour at the prospect of revenge on those who had injured him. 'Do as I say, Pedro, and you'll be the richest greaser this side of the border.'

Sam stared over the top of a boulder, his eyes thoughtful as he surveyed the terrain. He couldn't see anything of the men who were following him, but he didn't expect to. Among the rifts and gullies they could remain hidden for as long as they wished.

Carefully, making sure that the rifle did not ring against the stone, he crawled away from the camp-site. He climbed high so that he could look down and, nestling among a heap of boulders, he rested the rifle where he could get a clear shot at anyone coming up the trail towards where Pedro was making a great deal of noise at his cooking.

And then he waited.

He waited with the patience of a hunter, a born killer, a natural bush-whacker. He ignored the heat of the sun and the discomfort of the rocks on which he rested. His eyes, narrowed and feral, stared down the sights of his rifle and his finger, relaxed now, but ready at any moment to apply pressure to the trigger, was in position for a snap shot.

Time passed. Overhead in the clear blue of the sky the sun lowered itself past the zenith towards the horizon. Little sounds became magnified in the clear air and, from a long distance away, the sound of a coyote echoed thin and unreal from the hills around.

Something moved down along the trail. It was a hint of movement, nothing more, but as he saw it Sam tensed, his eyes narrowing to mere slits and his finger tensed as it caressed the trigger.

Again came the movement and, drifting like a ghost, soundless and almost inevitable as it blended with the rocks, a shape moved forward towards the camp-site.

Sam squeezed the trigger.

8

Grant was worried. He sat on his horse, the other two close to him, in the deep shelter of a canyon which crossed the path which they had taken to follow the outlaw and his guide. They had ridden far and carefully, circling and detouring, always trailing the two men as they wended their way deeper into the foothills.

'I don't like it,' he said. 'They've halted for too long.'

'You think they spotted us?' Joe looked anxious.

'I don't know.'

'They might have seen us cross the river,' said Holden, 'but we've kept pretty well hidden since then.' He shrugged. 'If you ask me we're worrying about nothing. Sam and that half-breed are probably cracking a bottle and making a ball out of it.'

'I don't think so.' Grant tilted his head and listened to the sounds coming from the camp. 'Listen, can you hear Sam talking at all?'

'No,' admitted Holden, 'but that means nothing. He'd make the greaser do the cooking while he sat and rested. Maybe they want to kill a little time or maybe Sam's fallen asleep.'

'You think this could be a trap, Grant?' Joe looked at the rocks around them. 'Is that it?'

'I'm working on what I'd do if I found some men following me,' said Grant slowly. 'The best thing would be to draw them out and shoot them down. The other alternative is to reverse the roles, us to track them instead of the other way about. From what I know of Sam I don't think he'd be interested in that. I've got the feeling that he's lying up there somewhere just waiting for a shot at us.'

'Aren't you over-rating him a little?' Holden shifted in his saddle. 'As I see it they've camped and are resting. That's all. If we ride a little closer we may even be able to look at them. Anyway, sitting here isn't doing us much good.'

'Maybe not, but let's not rush into anything,' said Grant. He frowned. 'All that noise is out of character. This is Indian country and they wouldn't want to advertise themselves any more than they have to. So why all the banging and talking?'

'Sound is magnified in these hills,' said Holden. 'Maybe they don't know just how much noise they are making.'

'Sam's no fool,' said Grant evenly. 'He's not a tenderfoot either. And if he was the guide isn't. That half-breed wouldn't make any more noise than a snake crossing a rock unless he wanted to. No, Dan, I don't like it. Something's wrong somewhere and I want to find out what it is.'

'How do you aim to do that? Ride up and join them?'

'If they know that we're following them then there isn't much else we can do. Sam isn't going to lead us to the hide-out if he can help it. Either he'll circle and hope to lose us, or he'll set an ambush to cut us down. I think he'll do the latter. He doesn't love us and in these hills a good shot could pick us off without trouble.'

Grant stared up at the hills again, his eyes thoughtful.

'This is what we do: I'll climb up and try to get above the camp. One of you circle around and get to the other side of where they are resting. The other one will stay here with the horses.'

'What good will that do?' said Holden. 'You can't search every inch of these rocks. If you tried crawling around you'd only show yourself and get shot.' He sucked in his cheeks. 'Someone's got to draw their fire.'

'All right, Dan, then this is how we do it: Take your rifle and get high but under cover. Joe, you do the same. When you're in position I'll head towards the camp. If they are resting then I'll be able to spot them. If not then I'll draw their fire.'

'And get killed?' Holden shook his head. 'There must be some other way.'

'There is,' said Joe. 'I'll draw their fire.'

'No.' Grant stared at them, his face hard. 'I'm not playing the hero for the fun of it. I've had experience at this sort of thing before and you haven't. I dodged bullets for four years, remember, and this is nothing to what I've been through in the past. Now move! We're wasting time.'

He waited until they had taken their rifles and moved off. He waited until he was sure that they were in position and then, slowly, he began to walk along the trail towards the camp.

It wasn't an easy walk.

Despite his training nerves jumped in anticipation of the sudden shock of lead. His eyes flickered from side to side as he moved forward, scanning every nook and boulder, roving up the hills and probing shadows. Somewhere up there a man was ready to send leaden death towards him. It wasn't a nice thought.

It was very quiet. Aside from the noises coming from the camp nothing disturbed the stillness of the air. Grant trod cautiously, trying to blend in with the rocks, trying to step on solid ground so that he would make no sound.

A stone clicked under his heel and he froze, standing like a thing of wood for a long moment as the sound died away. He stooped and, picking up a stone, threw it forward against the rocks so that it made a sharp sound. Again he waited then, as nothing happened, he moved forward, nerves tense, eyes watchful.

The sound of the shot rolled like thunder from the boulders around him.

It was shocking, that noise, magnified as it was by the stone. It slammed and rolled and sent echoes dinning through the clear air. More shocking was what happened just before the sound of the report drummed against Grant's ears. He gasped as something burned across the top of his left shoulder, searing with hot lead the tender flesh and, as the pain registered, he dropped and rolled and hid himself from the marksman.

The wound wasn't serious, a quick examination assured him of that and, after staunching the blood with his neckscarf he turned his attention to more important matters.

The noise from the camp had stopped. Pedro, or whoever it was who had made it, had heard the shot and was probably playing his own part in the drama. If anything it made the situation worse, for now, instead of one unknown gunman threatening them from the shelter of the hills, now there were two.

A second shot cut through the air, a third, and then a rolling volley of artificial thunder rolled and echoed from the hills. Grant, at the sound of the first shots, had flung himself forward along the trail, stooping and thrusting his long legs at the rocky ground. He dived towards the shelter of a boulder as lead sent chips of stone humming through the air and then, his own pistol in his hand, turned to stare up at the hills.

He caught a gleam of light, the sun reflected from the polished metal of a rifle barrel and, even as he saw it, his pistol added to the noise around him. Three shots he sent towards that gleam of light, three packages of leaden destruction and then, as he was taking more careful aim, something crashed against his back and sharp steel lanced towards his throat.

Luck saved him, luck and his own trained reflexes. He ducked, dropped his pistol and grabbed at a dirty wrist. Dirty that wrist might be but it rippled with muscle and was far from weak. Desperately Grant held on, twisting until the knife fell from nerveless fingers, and then, with every ounce of energy and strength in his body, stooped and sent his attacker spinning over his shoulder.

Pedro glared up at the tall man, tried to yell, then fell silent as Grant scooped up his gun.

'Yell and I'll kill you.' Grant licked his dry lips and leaned against a boulder. The struggle had wrenched his wound and his shirt was wet with blood. 'How many of you are there?'

'Two, señor.'

'Where is the other one?'

'You saw him, señor. You fired towards him.'

'Good.' Grant glared upwards to where he had seen the gleam of light. It had gone. Suddenly he became aware that it was very quiet. The shooting had stopped and, in the silence, Grant could hear the click of spurs and the scrape of boots as men walked towards him.

'Grant?' Holden jumped from the top of a rock. 'You all right?'

'Yes. Where's Joe?'

'Here.' Joe came towards them. He carried a rifle in one hand and his shotgun in the other. His face seemed strained and his clothing was flecked with blood.

'Sam?'

'Dead.' Joe didn't volunteer more

information and Grant didn't ask. He sagged a little, hardly conscious of gentle hands tending his wound and, when his vision had cleared, Joe had washed and bound the shallow groove in his shoulder. He became aware of the half-breed speaking with urgency.

'We go. We go fast. Too much noise. Too many Indians in these hills. They hear and come for us. We go now.'

'He's right, Grant,' said Holden tiredly. 'All that shooting is bound to attract attention. I'd say that we move away from here while the going's good.'

Grant stared at the gambler, remembering what he had said about being able to provide safe-passage through Indian country. Holden winked and lowered his voice:

'I know what you're thinking, but don't say it out loud. With Sam dead the only chance we've got of finding the hide-out is for the half-breed to take us. The trick is to make him do just that.' He raised his voice and snapped at the half-breed: 'You, what's your name?'

'Pedro, *señor*.'

'You were taking Sam to meet a big man called Jud. Is that true?'

'*Si, señor*.'

'Where is the place you were taking him, the hide-out?'

'Do you not know?' Something gleamed in the liquid dark eyes. Grant saw it and straightened from where he leaned against the boulder.

'Do not toy with us,' he rapped in Spanish. 'We give you a choice. Either you take us to the hideout or we leave you here for the vultures to eat and peck at your dead eyes. Well?'

'I am a poor man, *señor*,' whined the half-breed. 'You will pay me?'

'When we reach the hide-out, not before.'

'But you will pay me?'

'Yes.'

'*Gracias, señor*. The place you seek is a little arroyo deep in the hills. There is a cave and there the big man waits with his friends. They have many boxes with them, guns I think, and much gold. We

162

can reach it before dawn if we ride hard, but *señor*, we must ride soon.'

'Are you afraid of the Indians?'

'Who is not afraid of the Red Devils? Me, I am an honest man, *señor*. I burn many candles in the mission and give what I can to the poor, but, yes, I am afraid.'

'You have reason perhaps, to be so afraid,' said Holden grimly. 'There are tales of Indian scalps being sold to the Government of Mexico for many dollars each. Many such scalps are taken from the heads of Indians too drunk to fight to retain them.' He stepped forward, his face savage. 'You would have fear of the men you robbed. You would know what they think of such as you. Is that why you are afraid?'

Pedro sweated but did not answer. Grant stared at him for a long moment and then, with a curt gesture, led the way to the horses. Silently they mounted and rode along the trail.

'Is that true?' asked Joe after a while.

'Do they really buy Indian scalps?'

'The Mexican Government?'

'Yes.'

'They buy them right enough,' said Holden tightly. 'There's no love lost between the Apache and the Mexicans. The Indians despise them and in return the Mexicans hate the Indians. Maybe they have cause, the Indians think nothing of raiding across the border for food and blankets, horses and guns. But the Indians regard that sort of thing as a kind of game. Warfare to them isn't what it is to us. It is part of their tradition that they shall always be at war with one tribe or another. It gives the young men a chance to win fame and become a warrior with a squaw of his own and a feather in his hair.'

'But it is still war,' said Joe slowly. His face was thoughtful, as though he were trying hard to understand.

'Men die and widows are made,' said Holden, 'and, in that regard, it is not a good thing, I suppose. But you must remember that they don't look at it as we do. To go on a raid is a part of every warrior's upbringing, the thing he is trained for.' He sighed and stared down at his horse's ears. 'The Indians are a peculiar people, Joe, and they are a very proud race indeed. They have their own culture and it is a good one. There are things we do which literally horrify the Indians. We strike our children, for example, a thing they never do.'

'You mean that they do not correct their children when they do wrong?'

'They never strike their children,' repeated Holden. 'An Indian child is assured of all the love and comfort it requires. For the first three years of its life it is kept to a cradle board and carried with its mother wherever she goes. The mother comforts it, massages it, gives it continual affection. By that means an Indian child has a sense of security, of belonging, which children of our own culture do not have. No one, and I repeat that, no Indian is ever cruel to a child.'

'But what about the raiding parties

and the prisoners they take? They kidnap children, don't they?'

'Yes. On a raid the war party will kill warriors and take squaws and children as prisoners. But they don't regard them as slaves or as inferiors. For a time the women may be set to work as general servants but, after a while, they can marry into the tribe and are thought of as full members of that tribe. The children are brought up in exactly the same way as any other Indian child. If the children are orphans they are given to couples with few or no children of their own. This has happened many times before and even white children are so treated. There is more than one Indian warrior riding the plains with blue eyes and brown hair, children captured from the old wagon trains or settlements and brought up as full-blooded Indians.' Holden glanced towards Joe. 'There are some of your own colour too.'

'With the Indians?'

'Yes. Runaway slaves, mostly. Those

who headed north and were pushed west until they met up with the Indians. I've met a couple myself and there are many more.'

'Incredible!' Joe couldn't seem to grasp it. 'And they are treated as equals?'

'Yes.' Holden glanced around him and spurred his mount forward a little. 'You see, Joe, the Indian has no race or colour bar. It doesn't matter what the colour of a man's skin might be, what does matter is that he should be a man. Prove yourself to the Indians and they will treat you as an equal in every sense of the word. They really regard all men as their brothers and they mean it. I don't know what will happen to the released slaves now, I'd guess that some of them are in for a shock, but I could be wrong. One thing is certain, they'll never be treated as true equals by the white man as they would by the Indian.'

'You think that?' Joe bit his lip as he rode forward. He was no fool and he had both seen and heard much on his long ride with Grant. The Civil War had been triggered because the North refused to see eye to eye with the South on the question of slavery. To Joe and those like him the war had been a crusade with the victorious armies of the North coming to liberate the slaves of the South. The North had won the war and freed the slaves but, even now, the white men, both those of the North and the South, still regarded the coloured man as little more than an animal.

He dismissed the thought from his mind as Grant drew rein.

'What is it?' Holden rode forward and joined Grant and Pedro. 'Is something wrong?'

'I don't know.' Grant gestured to the half-breed. 'Pedro is worried about something.' He stared at the half-breed. 'What is it?'

'Indian sign.' Pedro sweated as he stared about him. 'I am afraid, *señor*. I have the impression of eyes, too many eyes. This is a bad place.'

'Then get us out of here.' Grant patted his restless horse. 'Head for the hide-out and we'll be safe. Hurry.'

★　★　★

'Maybe we should go back,' muttered the guide. His swarthy face glistened with perspiration and his eyes rolled as he tried to stare in every direction at once. Grant frowned, not understanding the man's sudden fear, and, as Holden moved forward a little, caught his arm.

'What is it, Dan? Do you know?'

'I'm not sure,' said the gambler slowly. 'I can't see anything but that means nothing. There could be Indians all around us for what we know. Pedro must sense something.' He stared at the guide. 'What is it, man? What do you see?'

'That.' Pedro pointed towards the ground. 'Horse droppings, still fresh. You see?'

'I see,' said Grant. His eyes narrowed. 'And no shoe marks. The

Indians ride unshod horses, don't they, Dan?'

'Mostly.'

'So a party passed through here recently.' Grant shrugged. 'They could be miles away by now.'

'No,' said Pedro. 'They are ahead of us or all around us.' He jerked at his rein. 'I go back. You ride on if you wish. You fools to ride on. I go back.'

'Hold it.' Grant slipped his pistol from its holster. 'Stay where you are. Move and I'll shoot!'

'Make a noise now and the Indians will find us all,' snarled the half-breed in Spanish. 'You can fight them if you wish, me, I go back now. Shoot if you dare.'

'Wait.' Grant jingled coins with his left hand. 'Tell us where the hide-out is and you can go with much gold. Refuse to tell me and I shoot you. Well?'

'I cannot tell you just where the hide-out is,' said the guide. 'You are strangers to this country, how would you know the trails? I can take you there but I cannot tell you the trails from here. You would not know the places I mean.'

He was right and Grant knew it. Unless the man could draw an accurate map verbal descriptions were useless. Even Sam, with his knowledge of the hills, had needed a guide to steer him on a roundabout route. Grant had even less chance of finding the hide-out than had Sam.

'Then you must take us,' he repeated. He cocked his pistol with a grim finality. 'You tried to kill me, Pedro. Don't think that I'll hesitate to shoot. I'll take my chances with the Indians if they come. Now, turn back and lead on. Move!'

For a long moment the half-breed hesitated then, because of the pistol or because of something in the tall man's voice, he turned and rode as he was bidden.

He rode slowly, his eyes never lifting from the path and behind him the others followed, nerves tense and their hands resting on their pistols. For perhaps an hour they rode, winding their way through a narrow canyon, the shoes of their horses slipping on weathered stone. Twice Pedro drew rein and stared at the ground, each time making as if to turn and each time continuing as he stared at the grim features of the tall man and his companions. The third time he stopped, desperation had given him strength.

'We go no further,' he said. 'Kill me if you must but rather your bullet than the fires and knives of the Indian squaws. To continue is to ride into death.'

'You are a fool,' said Grant emotionlessly. He stared at the guide and knew that no threat, no promise would drive the man further. 'You are a coward.'

'I am a coward,' said Pedro sullenly. 'Perhaps you would not be so brave if you had seen what I have seen. The Indians are not human. They have ways of making a man die and I have seen the results of such ways. Not for me, señor. Kill me if you must but I go no further.'

'And the hide-out?'

'I will tell you what I can. Ride this trail until you reach the mountain shaped like the head of a man. Turn east and ride for five miles. Then you will come to a little valley. From there you ride north and ride until you reach a clump of trees. The hide-out is in a cave at the foot of a hill five miles to the west of those trees.'

'Is that all you can tell us?'

'That is all.'

'If there are Indians watching us they will see you ride off alone,' said Holden easily. 'They will not hesitate to attack one man.'

'Nor four, señor. I take my chances.'

The guide scowled as he turned his horse and rode past them down the trail. He rode with fear at his elbow but, as he heard neither the whisper of a gun clearing leather nor the click of a cocked pistol, he gained courage. His shoulders straightened, his spurs dug into the flanks of his horse, his eyes regained their cunning.

Grant sighed as he watched him go. He felt no hate for the man, no contempt even, for he knew that the guide spoke from knowledge. But he knew too that they would never be able to find Jud from the scanty directions even if they were the true ones. Once they lost the guide they would he stranded in a literal wilderness.

He was still staring after the guide when the arrow lanced out of nowhere and buried itself in Pedro's shoulder.

9

There was no warning. Even as Grant snatched his gun from his belt and dived from his horse to the shelter of a boulder he found time to wonder at the utter absence of warning. There had been nothing but the arrow lancing from out of thin air, the guide's scream as the barbed head bit deep, then a shocking chorus of war whoops and yells.

Grant fired at a painted shape, thumbing back the hammer ready to fire again then eased his finger from the trigger as Holden jumped before him.

'Hold your fire, Grant,' the gambler yelled. 'Joe! Hold your fire! Leave this to me.' He stepped forward, arms outflung, and yelled something in a language Grant didn't understand. Holden called out, paused, then called again.

'Can they understand you?' Grant rose from his shelter, his gun loose in his hand. He stared around him at the painted faces of the warriors, assessed the odds, then slipped the gun back into its holster. 'Joe,' he called softly. 'Put away your gun. If we try to shoot our way out they'll cut us down. Better leave this to Dan.'

'You're showing sense, Grant,' said the gambler. 'Shoot now and you won't stand a chance.' He lifted his arms and called again.

'What are you saying?' asked Grant.

'I'm telling them that we are friends,' said Holden curtly. 'I'm calling them brother and telling them that I belong to the Arapahoe.'

'Will they believe you?'

'They will if they give me a chance to convince them.' Holden fell silent as a tall, feather-bedecked warrior came up to him. Grant stared at the Indian with interest.

He was tall, as tall as Grant himself, with a sunburned skin and aquiline features. His eyes were deep set and his mouth betrayed a nature both ruthless and just. Search as he might Grant could detect no traces of weakness or bestiality such as were so often to be found on the faces of men of his own race. This Indian might be a savage compared to modern civilization, but he was a man for all that.

His face was streaked with red and yellow, his trousers fringed and beaded. He wore a leather jerkin, ornamented with strangely shaped bead-work designs and bright with pigments. His head-dress was a simple band supporting seven feathers. In his left hand he held a coup stick, a long thin shaft ornamented with feathers, each feather a token of some battle or raid in which he had participated. At his waist hung a belt, supporting knife and tomahawk. A quiver was slung over his shoulder full of arrows and a bow, strung and ready for use, also hung from his neck. He carried a rifle in his right hand and, looking at it,

Grant felt himself go tense with anger.

It was a good weapon, new, brightly shining, twin to the one he himself owned. It was a better weapon than any of the Confederate Army had carried in the field of conflict, a magazine Winchester, a repeating rifle such as had been perfected at the end of the Civil War. No trade gun this, but a precision weapon capable of killing a man up to a range of at least two hundred yards.

He became aware that Holden was talking rapidly in the unknown language.

The chief listened, nodded, said something in the same tongue. Holden gestured and spoke at greater length. He swept his hand from the sky down to the earth and back to the sky. He pointed at Grant and at Joe, gestured to the groaning guide who lay, crouched and whimpering with the pain of the arrow embedded in his shoulder. He ceased talking, folded his arms, and stared the chief directly in the eyes.

'It is well,' said the Indian in English. He spoke with an awkwardly slurred accent and Grant guessed that he had learned the language from the settlers and traders. 'You are our brother and these are your brothers, Black Face and Grey Eyes. But the Mexican is not your brother. He shall die.'

'There is a thing we would know before he dies,' said Holden quickly. 'It would be well for him to live until he tells it.'

'Speak,' said the Indian. Holden glanced at Grant, cleared his throat, then went into the guttural Arapahoe language. The Indian lifted one hand.

'You talk our tongue and it is well. But your brothers know not our tongue and what you say affects them and they must listen.' He paused. 'First hear me. For many miles we have watched and followed you. For many miles we waited for you to lead us to the place you are making for. Now you are ours to do with as we wish.'

179

'No,' said Grant. He stepped forward. 'You can make me do nothing. You can force me to do nothing. We came to this land in search for something. The man you wounded knows where that thing is. He is a bad man.'

'As was the one your brother with the black face killed,' said the Indian impassively. 'He too was a bad man.'

Grant said nothing. He was startled to learn that nothing they had done had passed unnoticed by the Indians. They must have watched and followed the white men from the moment they had crossed the river.

The Indian lifted the rifle in his right hand.

'This I tell you,' he said. 'White men came among us and promised us many sticks which shoot fire. These we desired because with them we could kill game and drive the white men from the land they told us was ours and then robbed from us. In return these men wanted the yellow stone we find in our rivers. They wanted much of this yellow stone and, in that, I think that they are mad. For what use can this yellow stone be to any man? Yet they desired it and to them it was given.'

'And the guns?' whispered Grant.

'They gave us some of the guns,' admitted the chief. 'They gave us a few and promised more when we had brought to them more of the thing which they call gold. This I would not do. We made a bargain for these guns and these men must keep that bargain. They have their gold and now we must have our guns.'

'Then why not take them?'

'These men are clever. We do not know where they hid the guns. It was to find out that we watched and waited by the river. A man with hair on his face knew the path, he we waited for, he it was you killed.'

'Jud's trying a double-cross,' said Holden. 'He's given out a few guns, just enough to make the Indians want more, but if he thinks that he can hold them to ransom he's made a big mistake.'

'What can they do?' asked Grant. 'They've paid over all their gold and now they've got to wait until Jud delivers the goods. If they start anything they'll lose the guns and gold both.'

'Gold means nothing to these people,' said Holden. 'But to them their word is sacred. If Jud tries to break his bargain they will kill him. The fool must think that he's dealing with Mexicans or white men, he doesn't know his own danger.'

'What about us?' Grant stared at the painted faces around him. A little way away the guide still groaned from the pain of the arrow in his shoulder. Joe, his eye thoughtful, stared at the Indians around him. Holden shrugged.

'As yet we are safe. Whether we can stay that way depends on a lot of things. Don't forget that the Indians are on the warpath and we're their enemies. I've got the edge on you because I'm a tribal member and so far they've permitted you to live because you're my friends. But don't hope for too much from that friendship. These warriors are itching to collect scalps and, if they decide to take yours, I won't be able to stop them.'

'Fair enough.' Grant looked thoughtful. 'As I see it the Indians want to find the guns. I want to find Jud and his boys. Find one and we find both. Right?'

'Yes. But our job is to keep those guns away from these Indians. If that means that Jud gets away with anything then that's just too bad, but he'll have to be allowed to do it.'

'No,' said Grant. 'Jud isn't going to get away.' He stepped forward towards the Indian chief and Holden caught his arm.

'What are you going to do, Grant?'

'Pedro knows where Jud is hiding. I aim to make him tell me.'

'Are you crazy! Do you want these Indians to get their hands on those guns?'

'That's a different problem,' said Grant coldly. 'I've ridden a long way to find Jud and I'm not going to give up now.' He stared at the gambler. 'Look at it this way. These Indians will find Jud sooner or later. They'll find him and torture him and he'll give them the rifles. If we don't act willing then they'll kill us and then find the guns anyway. I want to find Jud before I die.' He turned at that and spoke to the Indian chief:

'We are your friends, I want you to believe that. I know that you are at war with our people but you are a man and we are men and we can talk as men talk and not as cowards.'

'Speak,' said the Indian impassively.

'You seek the man called Jud and so do I. He has done me great wrong and I would kill him for that. We have a feud which can be settled only in blood. You understand that?'

The Indian nodded. He understood only too well for, among his people, blood feuds were common. So recognized was the right of one man to settle his score with another that the right of combat was given preference over all else.

'I understand,' he said.

'Good.' Grant took a deep breath. 'I would not die until I have met this man. The guide, the man you have wounded, knows where he is to be found.'

'The Mexican?' The Indian turned and called something to a painted warrior. The brave smiled, stooped over the moaning man, and swiftly cut out the barbed head of the arrow. Pedro screamed, twisted, then fell silent, his eyes wide with the fear of imminent death. The Indian chief stared down at him, then looked at Grant.

'He will guide us,' he said calmly. 'He will live until he shows us where this man lies hidden. After that he dies.'

'How?' Grant knew that he couldn't argue as to whether Pedro should live or die. The Indians and the Mexicans were old enemies and neither give nor expected quarter.

'He will die as a man should die,' said

the Indian calmly. 'If he guides us to the place where the guns are hidden he will have an easy passing. If he does not . . .'

Grant nodded, feeling the sweat of fear begin to bead his forehead. For a moment he had imagined that he had been talking to white men with their culture and settled treatment of prisoners. The words of the chief had reminded him that he was the prisoner of the Apaches, the war-like Indians who thought nothing of death and less of torture. Pedro was lucky in that he would be granted a clean death.

★　★　★

They came to the hide-out when the moon had set and starlight softened the harsh outlines of the hills around them. It had been a long and tedious ride with the guide swaying and mumbling prayers as he sat in his saddle, a warrior at each side to support him. Pedro was almost sick with fear and desperately anxious to please his painted captors.

He pointed with one shaking hand towards the shadow of a small canyon.

'In there,' he whispered. 'At the end there is a cave and there too are the things you seek.'

'Are there guards?' Grant rode towards the guide. He had not been disarmed and still carried his knife and pistol with the rifle in his saddle scabbard. He pressed forward, hoping against hope that he would be able to save the life of the half-breed, but he was too late.

Pedro half-turned to answer the question, stiffened, then slumped from the saddle. Behind him one of the Indians lifted his tomahawk, the bright blade now dull and stained, and wiped it on the mane of his horse. The job done, he slipped from his mount, tucked away the tomahawk, and reached for his scalping knife.

Grant swallowed and looked away.

Silently, like ghosts, several warriors slipped from their horses and disappeared into the starlit shadows. They moved with incredible stealth, slipping lightly over the rocky ground. For a while the rest of the party waited, sitting motionless on their horses then, appearing seemingly from the stone itself, an Indian whispered to the chief.

'They got the guards,' translated Holden to Grant. 'Two of them. The warrior reports that Jud and the rest of the gang are inside the cave.' He looked oddly at the tall man. 'There are a lot of boxes in there too.'

Grant shrugged.

Softly the Indians moved forward. The small canyon opened at the end to a rocky valley and, leading the way, the Indian messenger paused by the side of a thin opening. From behind that opening came a fitful gleam of light and the sound of muted voices.

'I'm scared, Jud,' said a thin, high-pitched voice. 'These Indians are the very devil to mess about with. Why not give them the guns and let's get away from here.'

'That's right, Jud,' said a heavier

voice. 'Tiny's right. Let's deliver the goods and pull out while we've still got our scalps.'

'Shut your mouth, the pair of you,' snarled a deep voice. 'You turning chicken on me like that fancy gambling man?' Jud chuckled. 'When Sam gets back we'll know just what to do. Don't worry about the Indians, they want these guns so bad they'll do anything to get them. The gold they gave us is nothing to what we can get if we play this thing right. Why pull out now when we can all make our pile? Quit whining and pass the bottle.'

Grant sucked in his breath as he heard the voices and his hand, hanging at his side, closed over the butt of his gun. These were the men he had trailed for months, the men who had burned his home and murdered his parents. They were here, before him, and hate like a burning river flooded through him and turned him from a man into a living instrument of destruction.

He stepped forward, the pistol

189

clearing its holster, his thumb pulling back the hammer as the muzzle centred on the belly of the big, scarfaced man.

'Jud,' he said, and his voice sounded like that of a stranger. 'You don't know me, Jud, but I'm going to kill you.'

His finger closed on the trigger.

10

Grant had forgotten the Indians. He had forgotten everything but his hate and his desire to kill the man who stood before him, to send hot lead smashing into yielding flesh, to turn the gun on the others, to fire and kill until the cave had become a shambles and his revenge complete.

Even as he squeezed the trigger a lithe brown arm snaked forward and knocked aside the weapon. Lead screamed as it ricochetted from the stone walls of the cave and the sound of its passing was lost in the general boiling of noise. Jud cursed, his hands darting to his own weapons. The fat man, Tiny, shrieked something and dived for a rifle. Kent, crouched and viperish, swore and clawed at his belt. Then the cave was full of Indians, yelling, painted, looking in the lamplight like a horde of devils as they rushed forward and overpowered the white men.

Disarmed, surrounded by the lances of their captors, they stood and glared at each other and at the Indians. Jud was the first to recover his assurance.

'Why, if it ain't my old friend Red Cloud,' he said, and held out his empty hands to the Indian chief. 'I'm sure glad to see you. I'd have liked it better had you come without that wildcat,' he darted a look of hate towards Grant, 'but you're welcome at any time.'

Red Cloud said nothing.

'I was aiming to contact you,' continued Jud. 'I was waiting for Sam Roper to ride in and let me know something. Then I was going to send up smoke so as you and your braves could come and collect the guns you paid for.' Jud grinned and waved his hands at the boxes around him. 'Here they are, Chief, all of them. Brand new and better than anything you could buy from anyone.'

'Sam won't be riding in,' said Holden

coldly. 'You shouldn't have sent him down to kill me, Jud.'

'Kill you?' The big man looked surprised. 'Why, Dan, I wouldn't do a thing like that. Why should I want you dead? We're in this thing together, ain't we? Right in all the way.' Jud licked his lips. 'We was only talking about you a while ago, ain't that right, Tiny?'

'That's right.' The fat man was streaming with perspiration. He looked somehow grotesque in his rough clothing and Grant knew that he would be more at home on one of the river boats or dealing faro in a saloon. Kent, the third man, remained silent, but his eyes flickered from side to side as he watched everyone and everything. He stared for a long time at Grant, a longer time at the dark features of Joe, and then he nodded as if solving something to himself.

'You said that Sam wouldn't be riding in,' said Jud. 'Accident?'

'Shotgun went off and hit him in the face,' said Holden coldly. 'We didn't bury him.'

'That's good news,' said Jud savagely. 'Fred Roper will be mighty pleased to hear about the way you treated his brother. Mighty pleased.'

'They can talk about it in Hell,' said Grant abruptly. 'If Fred was one of those two guards you set you won't be seeing either of them any more. You're on your own, Jud. All on your own.'

'What's riding you, stranger?' Jud stared at the tall man. 'I don't know you and you don't know me. Why come in here and try to kill me?'

'I'm paying off a few debts, Jud,' said Grant tightly. 'Maybe you wouldn't remember a time down South when you and your friends lit yourselves a fire and murdered a couple of old people who had welcomed you.' He stepped forward, his face a living mask of hate. 'Remember, Jud? A mansion down South and you dressed all in blue. You wanted gold and tortured a woman to make her husband tell you where he'd hidden it. There wasn't any gold, Jud, but you wouldn't take that. So you torched the house and shot the old man. Remember, Jud?'

'I know him,' said Kent suddenly. 'That darkie, I know him.'

'You should,' said Grant savagely. 'He was the man who welcomed you and fed you. He was the man you knocked down and kicked.' He strained forward against the arms which held him. 'That was my home you burned, Jud. That was my mother you tortured, my father you shot. Now you know who I am. Now you know why I'm going to kill you.'

'Talk,' sneered the big man. 'Big talk.'

'Good talk,' said Red Cloud suddenly. 'Blood feud. You fight.'

'Why not?' Jud shrugged. 'But that can come later. Right now we've a deal to settle. These are your rifles, Chief, and I'm glad you came to take delivery. You want more?'

'Yes.'

'Sure you do, lots more, and the bullets to go with them. Well, I can get you more. That is I can get them for you if I'm alive to do it. Maybe you'd better knock this wildcat on the head and get him out of the way. Maybe I can kill him, maybe not, but one thing's for sure. If he lives to spread the word you'll have all the United States Cavalry sweeping through these hills and burning your villages. If you want to make the most of these guns you'll have to wait until every brave has one of his own. Then you can really go to town.'

'That's right,' said the fat man desperately. 'This stranger is trying to cross you up, Chief. He doesn't want you to have the guns at all. He wants to see you lose your lands and be herded into the reservations. He's dangerous.'

'Am I dangerous?' Joe moved forward as far as the lance-points would permit. 'Kill Grant if you wish but while I remain alive none of you are safe. Do you think that I can ever forget what you did that night?'

'Hark at that bastard,' sneered Kent. 'Watch your mouth, slave, or I'll take a whip to your hide.'

'The last man who called Joe a slave,' said Holden casually, 'died back in Alamatri. You eager to follow him, Kent?'

'I ain't afraid of no darkie,' snarled the little man. He twisted his head and stared at the chief. 'This is getting us nowhere. If you want the rifles take them and get moving. If you want more then you'd better play things our way. Make up your mind.'

It was a mistake, and Grant knew it. The little man had revealed his true feeling and the Indians, while remaining impassive, had learned just in what regard they were held by these white men. Red Cloud, his face expressionless, stared from one to the other. He began talking in his own tongue.

'What's he saying?' asked Grant to Holden. The gambler listened then began translating.

'He's appealing to the warriors. He's telling them what there is between you and Jud. He is asking them what they wish to do.'

'Asking them?' Grant's voice echoed out his surprise. 'But he's the Chief. Why doesn't he just order them to do what he thinks best?'

'No Indian can order another Indian to do anything he doesn't want to do,' explained Holden. 'Even the chiefs are elected and can be deposed. The Council is usually made up of the elders of the tribe and they govern policy. But if a warrior wants to go on the war-path, then he'll do it, even if he has to go alone. Conversely, if he wants to quit fighting and go home, then he'll do that too. The Indians do not have any discipline as we know it. They have no punishments for anyone doing wrong. The worst punishment they can inflict is to expel a man from his tribe. He has to take what is his and leave the village. No other member of the tribe will acknowledge him. It's a sort of exile from his own kind. But they can't imprison each other, or force each other to do anything. An Indian will only take orders while he's willing to take them.'

'Odd.' Grant, used to the iron discipline of the Confederate Army, shook his head as he thought about it. 'How can these people ever hope to win a war against the white man while they act like that? Don't they realize that they are bound to be beaten?'

'They know,' admitted Holden. 'That is, the chiefs and elders know. The hot-blooded braves think they can sweep the white man back into the sea but that is just talk. You see, Grant, the Indians don't fight as we do. They go on the war path and have a few battles, running fights mostly, or skirmishes. To them those fights are a war. They cannot understand our single-minded purpose in warfare. They cannot or would not have a large standing army. They cannot and will not accept the discipline necessary in order to have such an army. The Indians are both blessed and cursed with a high individualism. Blessed because it makes them respect each other and cursed because it divides them among themselves. There are economic factors involved, a man can't fight all the time when he has to prepare for the winter. If he stays away from home too long his wife and children will suffer from want of food.'

'Starve, you mean?'

'No. No one family will ever see another go short of food while they have some to spare. There is no greediness or avarice in the Indian. But any warrior who neglected his family would be scorned and jeered at and made to feel small. None of them want that.'

'I see.' Grant nodded, interested in what he was learning. Joe was interested too, he moved a little closer to the gambler.

'Then the Indians can't possibly win any war with the white man?'

'No.' Holden sighed. 'They can see it as plainly as we can. Never forget that all the uprisings have been caused by our breaking of treaties. Further north the buffalo hunters are slaughtering the herds and robbing the Indians of their food supply. Without buffalo the Indians must raid across the border for cattle. That results in reprisals and more bloodshed. The Indians are hunters, they have no cattle of their own and they are not farmers. Take away the buffalo and they will starve.'

'But if they all got together,' suggested Joe. 'If they elected one chief and all obeyed him, what then?'

'If they could do that then they would still be beaten,' said Holden. 'But should they unite then they would set fire to the entire West. They would freeze transport, harry the settlers, cut off the troops. They know this country and they would cut us down. It would take years to hunt them down and thousands of lives would be lost. That is the dream of Sitting Bull and other great chiefs, but they think a little deeper than that. If they should unite then it would be for the sole purpose of making themselves so strong that they would be able to dictate their own peace treaty.'

'And then?'

'Then it would be broken again and

the whole business start over.' Holden sighed. 'It's a mess whichever way you look at it, Joe. I can't see any solution to the problem, not while the white man continues to break his word and rob the Indians of their own land. If we aren't careful we'll wipe out the entire Indian culture. I — '

He broke off as Red Cloud finished speaking. For a moment there was silence then a warrior, painted and feathered, said something. Another repeated it, a third, then all the rest together. Red Cloud bowed his head.

'What did they say?' whispered Grant. 'What is the decision?' He looked at Holden's face. 'Bad?'

'Bad.' The gambler swallowed. 'While admitting your right to the blood feud yet the warriors say that you are not an Indian and so are apart from them. Jud and his men have smoked the pipe of peace with Red Cloud but you have not. Also, they want the rifles. They want them so badly that they are willing to do as Jud suggests.' Holden shrugged.

'You can't blame them too much. Those rifles mean everything to the young braves. With them they think that they can re-win the West.'

'And Red Cloud?'

'He knows better. He doesn't trust Jud and he doesn't like him. But he isn't willing to turn against him because of you. After all, Grant, you are a white man and an enemy.'

'I showed him the way to get here,' said Grant. 'I could have kept quiet about Pedro. If it hadn't been for us Red Cloud still wouldn't have had the rifles.'

'Admitted.'

'Look, Dan,' said Grant. 'I'm going to kill Jud. I don't care what happens to me afterwards, but I'm going to kill Jud. Can you fix that?'

'I don't know.'

'If Red Cloud and the braves think that Jud is double-crossing them, what will happen?'

'Unless Jud delivers what he has been paid to deliver, they will torture him and the others to death.' Holden stared at Grant. 'What's on your mind?'

'Those rifles.' Grant squinted at the boxes. 'Where did you get them?'

'I told you, from the makers. I paid in gold for delivery in Mexico.'

'And ammunition?'

'Some. The big shipment of ammunition was the one I refused to arrange. That is why Jud sent Sam after me. Rifles are useless without bullets and Jud knows it. He aims to sell the rifles and then charge more for the bullets. That's why he's feeling so safe.' He stared at Grant. 'You've got something on your mind.'

'So those guns have no ammunition with them?'

'Sure they have, not much, but a little.' Holden shook his head. 'It won't work, Grant. The Indians aren't children, they know all about rifles. You can't tell them that they won't work.'

'Can't I?' Grant took a deep breath. 'You've been outsmarted, Dan. Or maybe you just didn't care. Didn't you think those rifles came cheap?'

'Sure, but why not?' The gambler shrugged, cynically. 'I was in it for the business. I told you that. At first all I wanted was the chance to help the Indians and the money I got for doing it. Later I felt differently about it, but that's no good now, it's too late.'

'No it isn't, Dan. Those rifles are good weapons, sure, but they aren't what you think they are. They are surplus war stock, not the late-model repeaters I thought they were. The gun Red Cloud is carrying never came from that batch.'

'Maybe not,' said Holden thoughtfully. 'Jud brought a few cases on his own and arranged for me to buy the rest. The ones I bought came cheap as you said.' Holden looked alarmed. 'What's the matter with them, they're rifles aren't they?'

'Yes, Dan, but they are Confederate rifles.'

'So?'

'They have a different bore, Dan. The

ammunition we carry won't fit those guns. Now do you get it?' Grant smiled for the first time since entering the cave. 'Red Cloud isn't going to like being cheated. All he knows is that his own bullets won't fit those guns. Any brave carrying one can't get more ammunition from the settlers or cavalry. They won't like having to rely on Jud for their bullets, not when Jud wants so much gold in exchange.' Grant nodded as he thought about it. 'A neat scheme, Holden, a very neat scheme. Supply the Indians with weapons and then hold them to ransom for the ammunition. Jud was clever to think of it. Or did he think of it?' Grant stared at Holden. 'Or was it that you tried to be clever too?'

'I asked for repeating rifles and ammunition,' said the gambler sickly. 'I got what I asked for. I didn't stop to think about the bore.' He swallowed. 'If they find out I did it they'll kill me.'

'Yes,' said Grant slowly. 'They will, won't they?'

'What can I do, Grant?'

'There's only one thing you can do,' said the tall man evenly. 'Throw the blame on Jud.' He looked at the Indians around him. 'In a way it's worked out for the best. Without ammunition those rifles are useless. They won't be used to kill the settlers and set the West on fire with fresh Indian wars.' He looked at the Indians again. 'Better tell them, Dan, and tell them fast.'

He smiled as the gambler spoke to Red Cloud.

11

The Indians took the news calmly enough. They did not rave and scream and display their emotion but Grant, watching them, knew how they felt. They had been robbed, they had no other word for it. They had been tricked, made to feel like children, and they wanted revenge on the men who had done it.

Jud tried to bluster. He opened case after case and tested rifle after rifle. He loaded one with the ammunition supplied and fired it and the Indians nodded. Then they tried to fit their own bullets into the weapons and failed. They tried with their own guns and the bullets fitted but the Confederate rifles would not accept the larger shells they carried.

Then they put down the guns and stared at Jud.

'Don't worry about it,' said the big man. 'I've got ten million rounds of ammunition coming up this way. Enough bullets for all the guns and more to spare. Just give me time to get them, that's all I ask. Just give me time.'

'You speak with a forked tongue,' said Red Cloud coldly. 'You gave us guns and said that the rest of the guns would be as those you gave us. Much of the yellow stone we gave you for these rifles and they are of no use to us. We want guns the same as the long knives carry, the soldiers, and the ones we have. You have lied to us and treated us like children. You must die.'

'No!' Jud strained against the hands which held him. He stared at Grant. 'You! You did this. Tell them the truth, damn you. Tell them that these are good guns and that there is plenty of ammunition for them. Tell them that everyone will be carrying the bullets to fit these guns soon. Tell them!'

Grant shook his head.

'You, Holden. You tell them. Damn

it, man, it's all your fault. You bought the rifles and arranged for the ammunition. You're as much to blame in this as I am. More, I trusted you, curse you, and you've let me down. Talk to the chief and tell him that. You talk their dog-lingo. Tell them the truth.'

Holden shrugged.

'Look, Chief,' said Jud desperately. 'I never meant to cross you. I'm your friend. I was going to give you the guns and ammunition at the same time. You've got to believe me, Chief. You've got to believe me.'

'He lies,' snapped Grant. 'I can prove he lies. I challenge him to single combat. If he is telling the truth then Manitou will give him strength and he will kill me. If he does you will know that he is speaking without a forked tongue. If I kill him then he lied and his friends lied with him.'

Grant spoke again before Red Cloud could answer.

'If this man wished you well would he not have given you the guns? Would he have waited until you sought him out? Even now, long after he has taken your gold, still he has not the bullets for these guns. Before he will give you the bullets he will want you to give him more gold. Is that the way of a friend? Is that the way the traders deal with your people?'

'It is not,' said Red Cloud. He lifted his left arm and his coup stick sliced through the air. 'He must die.'

'He dies!' A warrior, painted like a devil, his scalping knife in his hand, screamed and flung himself towards the big man.

'No!' Grant surged forward and knocked the brave aside. 'He dies, yes, but at my hand.' He glared at the Indians. 'It is my right.'

'A deal!' Jud, his scarred cheek glistening with sweat, stared at the chief. 'I agree to fight this man in the Indian manner. If he dies we go free. If I die then Tiny and Kent are yours to do what you like with.'

'Like hell!' snapped Kent. 'What is this?'

'It is well,' said Red Cloud. 'All shall stand by one. If Grey Eyes wins, then the fat man and the small man die at the stake. If Scar-Face wins then Black Face and Onenonga, he who is white and yet of us, shall die also. I have spoken.'

And that was that.

Holden gave rapid advice as Grant prepared himself for the battle. The Indians had cleared a wide circle in the middle of the cave, piling the boxed rifles high to one side. They had added to the fitful gleam of the lantern with two fires, one at each end of the cave, and now stood in a circle, their faces inwards, their weapons in their hands.

'This is the drill,' whispered Holden. 'You'll be stationed one at each side of the circle. Two knives will be placed in the centre between you. At the word you both make for the knives and do your best to kill each other.' He whistled as he examined the wound on Grant's shoulder. 'You may have trouble with this.'

'I'll remember it.' Grant rubbed his wrists, arms and chest with grease from a bowl an Indian held out to him. 'Any rules?'

'None. Any trick you know is accepted. Fight as dirty as you know, the only thing is to win.' Holden hesitated. 'It's more than your life, Grant, you know that.'

'I know.'

'Make it fast then. That wound will break open and you'll lose a lot of blood. You know how to knife-fight?'

'I think so.'

'Watch his boots.' Holden swallowed. 'I ain't a praying man, Grant, but this is one time I wish I knew some words to help you.'

'Thanks.' Grant stepped forward into the circle. Red Cloud raised his arms, hesitated, dropped them.

The fight was on.

It started with a rush with both men diving for the knives which, their razor-edged blades gleaming in the light, rested on the rock at the centre of the cave. Even as he thrust himself forward Grant was evaluating his chances. His hate had left him now to be replaced by a cold determination. He was going to kill Jud, nothing else mattered but that.

He reached the knives a trifle late, a split second after the big man and, as he saw what had happened, he deliberately slowed down. Jud, intent only on grabbing at the blades, was unaware of his danger until too late. Grant, poising himself, kicked out his foot at just the right moment and Jud, his nose streaming blood, staggered back. Quickly, before Jud could recover, Grant stooped and snatched up his knife.

The Indians hummed in approbation at what they considered a clever trick.

Grant heard it and lost his sense of shame. This wasn't a clean fight. This was a fight on which hung the lives of three men and nothing he could do would be considered bad. He had won a point by his shrewd kick, now he had to follow his advantage.

He held his knife like a sword, thumb to the blade, the point upwards. In this position, the accepted knife-fighter's position, he could use the blade to thrust, cut and slash as well as parry. Now he advanced towards Jud, his body tense, poised on the balls of his feet like a dancer. He advanced and feinted towards the big man's eyes. He slashed, moved in and felt steel rip across his ribs.

And knew that he was hopelessly outclassed.

Jud was fast. Jud was desperate. Jud was experienced in what he did. The kick to his face had stunned him a little but now his senses were clear and his little eyes gleamed with hate as he stared at the tall man before him. He grinned as the knives met, his left hand darted out to slip on the greased skin of Grant's left arm. He twisted and his blade whined through the air in a vicious slash. He missed as he expected to but, instead of trying to fight his momentum, he spun on his heel, the knife an arcing thing of death before him so that he came on at Grant with shocking speed.

Luck saved the tall man, luck and instinct. He stepped back, desperately, and again he felt the burning kiss of steel as it gashed his skin across his chest. Blood mingled with sweat and grease and painted him with oozing colour.

Then he forgot he was a civilized man.

There is a state of mind essential to all those who fight and hope to win. They must forget everything but the task at hand, let all other emotions be overridden by the surging necessity to kill. They must forget even to think, to act by instinct, to use their bodies as nature intended and not slow down their reflexes by conscious thought. Grant reached that state when he felt the knife slash at his unprotected skin.

He made a sound, an animal sound deep in his throat and his eyes, normally clear and cold, became red and bestial. He thought of his home and the stench of burning. He thought of his parents and what this man had done to them. He thought of that and he went blood-mad.

He didn't feel the wound open on his shoulder and the blood run down his chest. He didn't know how he weaved and spun, parried and thrust, cut and slashed at the man before him. Once he felt the bite of steel in his left arm and felt his own right hand grow wet with something warm and sticky. Jud gasped as Grant's thrust went home but he was a big man, desperate, and the wound did not stop him. He stepped back, poised, and swung his heavy boot in a kick to the groin.

He missed. Grant caught the blow on his thigh and felt his leg grow numb. He staggered, almost fell, and then his left hand was clawing at the blood streaming from his shoulder.

He hopped forward and sent his knife in a ripping cut towards Jud's chest.

For a moment the two men stood, face to face, body to body, the eyes of one staring into the eyes of the other. Jud opened his lips and made a futile movement with his right hand, futile because Grant had trapped it against his side with his left arm.

'Damn you,' whispered Jud. 'Tricked me. Damn you.'

'You're going to die, Jud,' whispered Grant. 'Remember what you are dying for.'

He pulled out the knife and stepped away.

Jud stood and stared at him. For a moment the big man didn't move then, as a tree topples and falls, so he fell. His legs seemed to lose their strength. His eyes glazed. His body sagged and, slowly, he crumpled and sprawled head-long on the rocky floor of the cave.

'You did it! By Heaven you did it!' Holden came forward, smiling, his hands eager to staunch blood and dress wounds.

'For a moment there, Grant,' said Joe

feelingly, 'I thought that you was beat for sure.' He sucked in his breath. 'Man, I knew just how you felt.'

'Yes,' said Grant. He felt a little light-headed and the cave seemed to be revolving around him. 'You went through it too, didn't you, Joe?'

He straightened at the sting of something on his shoulder and chest. Holden was busy sponging the wounds and applying iodine. Around them the Indians were whooping and waving their weapons in excitement at the culmination of the fight and, to one side, Tiny and Kent stared about them with faces waxen with fear.

Grant looked at them and wondered why he felt no hate. They, equally so with Jud, had been responsible for the thing done to his home and parents. Now they were going to die by Indian vengeance instead of at his own hand. Now they were going to pay the full penalty for their crimes but he, the man who had trailed them for so long, no longer wanted any part of it. The trail had finished. Now he felt only tired and disgusted with it all.

Joe caught him as he staggered and almost fell.

'Steady, Grant,' said Joe. 'You've lost a lot of blood and must take things easy for a while.' He stared at where the other two white men stood surrounded by painted braves. 'The last two,' he whispered. 'When they are dead this thing is finished.' He looked at Grant. 'Are you satisfied?'

'At what?' Grant shook his head. 'What have I done? You killed Sam, not I. The Indians killed Fred Roper, I didn't. The Indians will kill Tiny and Kent. All I did was to kill Jud.'

'You killed Jud in fair fight, man to man,' said Joe. 'I'm glad it happened like that. I know you, Grant, better than you know yourself. You wouldn't have been able to rest ever again had you slaughtered men in cold blood. This way you have done your job. Now forget it and let things ride as they stand.'

'He's right,' said Holden. 'I've seen this thing happen before. A man takes the vengeance trail and then he's lost. He can't stop, Grant. He kills his man but then he finds that he's got to keep on killing. He changes from a man to a machine. He lives with hate and no man can do that and remain sane.' He stared at the Indians as they led their captives from the cave. 'Forget it now, all of it, and start leading your own life again.'

Grant nodded, he was thinking of an old priest and what that old man had told him. It was true. Now that the search was over and his wrongs avenged he felt a strange peace. He wondered if he would have felt that peace had he himself turned murderer.

He looked up to see Red Cloud.

The Indian stood before them, his eyes impassive, his arms folded across his chest. He looked at Grant, at Joe, at Holden, then back to Grant again.

'It was well done,' he said in his deep voice. 'Manitou gave your arm strength and your mind cunning. The big one is dead and his friends die very soon now. It is time for us to go.' He looked again at Holden. 'You, Onenonga, you who came among us and learned our ways and talk our tongue, will you go again?'

'Am I welcome in the wickiups of your people?'

'You are welcome. We know that your ways are not our ways and that you are filled with strange longings, but that is as Manitou wills. You are of us and we accept you.'

'It is well.' Holden glanced at Grant and hesitated. 'My friend is sick. He needs white man's medicine. Alone here he will die. I must take him to the place of the soldiers so that he can be made well again. He is a good man.'

'The long knives have built their wooden fort a day's ride from this place,' said Red Cloud. 'My braves shall ride with you to save you from harm.'

Grant tried to speak his thanks but Red Cloud was gone. Some warriors waited outside with the horses and they helped the tall man to mount. The night was cold but he did not feel it, already he was burning with fever from his wounds.

He never remembered much of that ride.

Holden rode at his left hand and Joe at his right and between them they steadied him in his saddle. Dawn came with a rush of red and gold, orange and amber, pink and silver blue. The trail opened on to a plain and, far in the distance, they could see the walls of the fort. The Indians had left them when they emerged from the hills though Grant guessed that they were waiting back there to escort Holden back to their village.

'Are you really going back with them, Dan?'

'Yes.' Holden rode silently for a while. 'I aim to help them, Grant. If I can just save them from a cheating trader then I shall feel that I've done something with my life. I guess that's about all I can do now.'

Grant nodded. He felt weak but his head was clear and he knew that he would soon recover.

'We may meet up again, Dan,' he said. 'I think that I'll stay in the West now that I'm here. What about you, Joe?'

'I'd like to go with Dan if he'll take me.' The man stared defiantly at Grant. 'What else can I do? I have no home, no race, no place to call my own. In the South I'm considered to be less than dirt, in the North a servant slightly higher than an animal. Only here, among the Indians, can I be accepted as an equal.'

'Is that your only reason, Joe?'

'No.' Joe looked thoughtful. 'I belonged to a minority, Grant, a slave, and I know what it is to take orders. The Indians don't know and yet they will have to learn. Unless they learn to take orders then the white men will exterminate them. We know it. They know it but refuse to admit it. Am I right?'

'Yes,' said Dan. 'They are a proud

people but unless they learn to bend then they will be broken.' He looked at Joe. 'You think that you can help them?'

'I think so. Maybe I can help them to learn to take orders. Maybe I can help them as you can, to teach the children a thing or two, Spanish perhaps or English, but I think that I can earn my keep. But the main thing is that I will be accepted as an equal.' He hesitated, looking at Grant. 'If that is all right with you, sir.'

It was the first time during all their journeyings that he had called Grant 'sir'.

'I don't own you, Joseph,' said Grant. 'You go and do what you think is right.' He smiled at them and then, alone, rode forward.

Ahead of him the fort came closer, closer, while behind him two figures galloped towards the distant range of hills.

Grant didn't turn to wave goodbye.

He knew that, one day, they would meet again.

We do hope that you have enjoyed reading this large print book.

Did you know that all of our titles are available for purchase?

We publish a wide range of high quality large print books including:
Romances, Mysteries, Classics
General Fiction
Non Fiction and Westerns

Special interest titles available in large print are:
The Little Oxford Dictionary
Music Book, Song Book
Hymn Book, Service Book

Also available from us courtesy of Oxford University Press:
Young Readers' Dictionary
(large print edition)
Young Readers' Thesaurus
(large print edition)

For further information or a free brochure, please contact us at:
Ulverscroft Large Print Books Ltd.,
The Green, Bradgate Road, Anstey,
Leicester, LE7 7FU, England.
Tel: (00 44) **0116 236 4325**
Fax: (00 44) **0116 234 0205**